The Advocate's Nightmare

Teresa Burrell

Silent Thunder Publishing

Edited by L.J. Sellers

Book Cover Design by Madeline

ISBN: 978-1-938680-44-1

Silent Thunder Publishing

San Diego

Dedication

To Maritza's Mexican Food, the best Mexican food and salsa
I've ever had! Thank you,
Carmen and family..

Acknowledgements

Thank you JP for your consultations throughout the book.

A special thanks to Susan Moore for the title of the book.

And My Loyal Beta Readers:

Beth Agejew
Linda Athridge-Langille
Vickie Barrier
Denise Bowman
Melanie Cardullo
Teresa Harden
Alisha Henri
Crystal Kamada
Sheila Krueger
Janie Livingston
Joy Lorton
MaryAnn Schaefer
Colleen Scott
Uma Van Roosenbeek
Denise Zendel

Also by Teresa Burrell

THE ADVOCATE SERIES

THE ADVOCATE (Book 1)
THE ADVOCATE'S BETRAYAL (Book 2)
THE ADVOCATE'S CONVICTION (Book 3)
THE ADVOCATE'S DILEMMA (Book 4)
THE ADVOCATE'S EX PARTE (Book5)
THE ADVOCATE'S FELONY (Book 6)
THE ADVOCATE'S GEOCACHE (Book 7)
THE ADVOCATE'S HOMICIDES (Book 8)
THE ADVOCATE'S ILLUSION (Book 9)
THE ADVOCATE'S JUSTICE (Book 10)
THE ADVOCATE'S KILLER (Book 11)
THE ADVOCATE'S LABYRINTH (Book 12)
THE ADVOCATE'S MEMORY (Book 13)
THE ADVOCATE'S NIGHTMARE (Book 14)
THE ADVOCATE'S OATH (Book 15)
THE ADVOCATE'S PHANTOM (Book 16)

THE TUPER MYSTERY SERIES

THE ADVOCATE'S FELONY

(Book 6 of The Advocate Series)
MASON'S MISSING (Book 1)
FINDING FRANKIE (Book 2)
RECOVERING RITA (Book 3)
LIBERATING LANA (Book 4)

CO-AUTHORED STANDALONE

NO CONSENT
(Co-authored with L.J. Sellers)

Chapter 1

Monday morning

San Diego Attorney Sabre Brown took a seat at the table in the courtroom between two men dressed in suits. When the clerk read the allegations, the defendant, a cold-eyed man, smiled slightly. Sabre's client seated next to her went nuts, lunging over her, knocking her down, chair and all. The file she was holding sailed across the room. The two men hit the ground at the bailiff's feet, who by then was standing over them. The judge exited the courtroom through the back door as other marshals poured in from every entrance.

Bob Clark, Sabre's best friend and colleague, was seated in Department One of the juvenile dependency courtroom behind Sabre. When the commotion started, he jumped up to help Sabre, but one of the marshals stretched out his arm, palm open, to stop him. "Stay, I've got this." He helped Sabre up as the others broke up the fight and escorted the men out the back door. Sabre's client was still shouting as they were escorted out.

Sabre straightened her slim-fitting skirt, ran her hand through her light brown hair, and picked up her file.

"Are you okay?" the marshal asked.

"I'm fine. Just a little shook up."

"Did you hit your head?"

"No. I went over sideways, so I didn't hit the bar." Sabre rotated her right arm to test it. "I'm a little sore, but I don't think anything is broken. Thanks." She walked through the gate to where Bob was standing.

He put his arm around her. "Are you sure you're okay, Sobs?" That was his nickname for her because of her initials—S.O.B.

"Really, I'm fine." She rolled her shoulder again, then took a seat in the back of the courtroom.

Bob sat next to her. "What the heck was that all about?"

"The guy who flew across the table, Grady Harn, is my client. His eight-year-old daughter was molested by the stepfather, Ritchie Stadler, the guy he attacked. I'm not sure what set Grady off. Of course, he's furious at the guy, but he seemed to be handling it pretty well up until now. Maybe hearing the allegations out loud was too much for him."

"It was more than that," Bob said. "The jerk, Stadler, couldn't hide his creepy thoughts about the girl. He smiled when the clerk read them. I saw it, so I'm guessing your client did too."

Sabre sighed. "I caught that too. I wondered if that was what did it."

"I don't blame the guy. I'd kill anyone who hurt my kid." Bob grinned. "And half the time, I don't even like him that much."

"You talk so big. You would be devastated if anything happened to CJ."

"You're right." Bob looked up and nodded toward the woman who had been sitting next to the defendant. "Is that the mother?"

"Yes."

"I'm guessing, since she was seated next to her husband, she chose to believe him over her daughter?"

"That's right. She's still with him, although the child seems to be pretty clear about what happened."

"Stupid people," Bob said. "There's the judge."

"Stay where you are," Judge Thomas said. "This will only take a minute." The tall, gray-haired, robed man sat down. "We're back on the record. This case will be continued until the afternoon. Ms. Brown and Mr. Blake, please talk to your clients prior to returning to this courtroom. You should have ample time. That concludes this hearing."

"Who's the attorney for the creep?" Bob asked.

"He's retained, and his name is Bob Blake. He's from Orange County."

"Have you been yanking his chain?"

"Not yet, but I will."

Chapter 2

Chapter 2

Monday morning

"Isn't that Crazy Carla?" Bob asked, as he and Sabre walked out of Department One.

"It can't be. What would she be doing here?" Sabre smiled. "And don't call her that. It's disrespectful."

"Yeah, yeah." Bob picked up his pace to get closer to the dark-haired woman leaning against the wall at the end of the hallway. "That's her, isn't it?"

"Yes. But how did you recognize her? You only saw her a couple of times and that was years ago."

"I never forget a face, especially the crazies. Besides, she's a very attractive woman. I don't forget those either."

"My brother always dated pretty women, but Carla was exceptional." Sabre thought about the time when Ron was dating Carla. She was crazy about him, and for a while Sabre thought Carla might become her sister-in-law. When Ron moved to Texas, Carla had a breakdown. Sabre visited her a lot in the facility and became the only one who could keep her calm.

"Why would she be here? Did she have a kid?"

"Not that I'm aware of."

Just then Richard Wagner, another attorney, approached them. "Can one of you take over a case for me? I'm on detentions, but I have a conflict."

"I'm sorry," Sabre said. "I have to see a delinquency client before his case this morning and reprimand a client who just went ballistic in court. Besides, I just picked up three new cases and they will all be intense," Sabre said.

"This one might be better suited for Bob anyway," Wagner said. "The petition is against the mother and she has some mental illness problems."

Bob looked over at Carla. "Is that her?"

"Yeah. How did you know?"

"Just a hunch." Bob reached out for the paperwork Wagner was holding. "I got this."

When Wagner walked away, Sabre said, "Look at the petition and see how old the child is."

"Are you afraid it might be your brother's?"

"No. Ron hasn't seen her in probably eight years."

Bob glanced at the petition. "Isn't Ron's middle name Adrian?"

"Yes." Sabre hesitated. "Why?"

"The child is a boy named Ronald Adrian Brown, Junior."

No! Sabre's mouth dropped open. She reached for the paperwork. "Are you serious?"

"No." Bob jerked the file back and laughed. "I'm pulling your leg. It's a four-year-old girl named Liberty."

"You're mean. Having someone in my family in the juvenile court system is my worst nightmare."

"*That's* your worst nightmare? Of all the things we see every day, *that*'s your worst nightmare?"

"I have a hard-enough time staying detached from my cases. I don't think I could do it if I was dealing with family."

Bob shook his head. "I think having your family in this court would be kind of funny."

"You wouldn't if it was *your* family."

"I'd find that hilarious."

"Go talk to your client," Sabre said. "I have to see a client in the custodial interview room." But first she walked over to

Carla and hugged her. They chatted for a few minutes about the past few years and about her daughter, then Sabre left.

~~~

Bob read through the detention report, then approached Carla. He explained that he was her court-appointed attorney and discussed confidentiality.

"I want my daughter back," Carla said. "She should be with me. Can you help me?"

"I'll do my best, but we have some hurdles to get over."

"I'm a good parent."

"Yes, it appears you are," Bob said. He tried to be diplomatic but didn't pull it off too well. "However, according to the report, your mental health issues go way back."

"I know. But I've been getting treatment and doing well, until...." She stopped and looked down at her feet.

Bob waited. When she didn't continue, he asked, "Were you trying to end your life when you took the pills?"

"I don't know." Carla hesitated. "I guess. I just felt like I wanted to go to sleep and never wake up again."

"You understand that puts your daughter at risk?"

"I know, but I'll get the help I need. I just have to make the monsters go away. I don't want them to get Liberty either."

Oh boy. "What do you mean by monsters?"

"They're big furry things, and they come mostly at night."

"What do they do?" Bob didn't know if she was serious, so he watched her facial expressions carefully.

"They hover over my bed and tell me I can't escape."

"So, they talk to you?"

"Sometimes. Mostly, they just hang around. I try to get away, but I can't."

"Do they physically stop you?"

"It's like they form a wall and I'm afraid to go through them." Without changing her expression, she said, "But that's not why we're here. What happens today?"
~~~

Bob explained the court procedure to her, then said, "I see that Liberty is in foster care. Do you have any family who could take your daughter until we can get her back?"

"I have an older sister who I know would take her, but she's in Africa on a safari right now."

"No other family, parents, grandparents?"

"My father died of a heart attack when I was seven. My grandparents and my little sister were killed in a car accident years ago."

"Is that when you were hospitalized before?"

"Yes. I had a breakdown. I was in twice. Three times, counting the most recent one."

"Where is Liberty's father?"

"I don't know."

"Do you *know* who the father is?"

Carla whipped her head around with a look of indignation. "Of course, I do."

"I didn't mean to offend you. But according to the report, the birth certificate reads *Unknown* for the father."

"I didn't want him involved. He loved me, but then he was gone, and I didn't want to force him back. And I didn't want him to take her from me."

"Do you think he would do that?"

"He might. Don't get me wrong. He's a really good guy, and he'd make a great father." She looked Bob directly in the eyes for the first time. "Can they force me to say who the father is?"

"No. But if they think you know, they'll keep asking. Depending on how your case goes, you may decide that Liberty is better with her father than in a foster home. That is, until we can get her back to you. This case could take some time."

"I'll think about it."

"Carla, have you been given any meds for the monsters?"

"Yeah. But they won't take them."

It sounded like a joke, but she looked serious, so Bob kept a straight face.

Chapter 3

Chapter*Monday morning*

Sabre sat down across from Grady Harn in the interview room at San Diego Superior Court, Juvenile Division. A thick plexiglass loomed between them. "You doing okay?"

"I've had better days, but everyone has been super nice to me. The bailiff said I should be released after the hearing this afternoon. He told me to apologize to the judge and be as humble as I can."

"That's good advice. Mike has worked with this judge a long time and he knows that he's pretty predictable. Although no one blames you for what you did, you can't go off on the defendant no matter what he did. Especially not in the courtroom."

"I know. I saw his smirk and I lost it." Grady's voice rose a notch. "Did you know he smiled when they read the petition?"

"I saw it, and so did several others, including my friend who was sitting in the back, as well as the minor's attorney and County Counsel. No matter how much we agree with you that he is disgusting, it still doesn't justify your actions. We're trying to get this child placed with you and that set us back a bit."

Her client rubbed his forehead. "Did I ruin my chances?"

"No. You have a lot going for you, but it will take a little longer than we planned."

"How much longer?"

"That depends on a lot of things. Primarily, you have to beat her mother in the race. So far, she's not leaving her husband, so that's in our favor."

"I just don't get it." He shook his head. "How can she stay with him after what he did?"

"Maybe she believes him."

"Over our daughter? That makes no sense." Grady took a deep breath. "He makes a ton of money, and he has given her the good life. We were struggling when we got married, and I couldn't give Heidi what she wanted. That was one of our biggest problems. She always complained about not having nice things. I was working two jobs, but it was never enough for her."

"You seem to be doing well now."

"I have a good job now, one that I like. I oversee the planning and building of city parks. I also pay a lot of child support. But Stadler's a big financial guy. And I don't think a very honest one, but he keeps her in a fancy car, a huge home in La Jolla, and pretty clothes. Maybe that's enough for her."

"I gave up a long time ago trying to figure out why people do the things they do. We just need to concentrate on you, and show the court that the best thing for your daughter is you."

"How do we do that?"

"Like Mike said, you start with apologizing to the court. You will likely be ordered into anger management classes and/or therapy. Whatever the department recommends or the judge orders, you do it. You have no past history of violence, and even your ex-wife claims you were never abusive and always a great father. You've had a good working relationship with Dakota's mother in your co-parenting, until the abuse by the stepfather." Sabre paused. Her client knew all this, but she was reassuring both of them. "Even if your ex-wife changes her story, it's going to look bad for her and not likely be believed. You must continue to have as much contact with

Dakota as the court will allow. You'll probably hear some objection to that this afternoon, but let me handle it. Do you understand?"

"I'll be on my best behavior. My daughter is the most important thing in my life."

Chapter 4

Monday noon

"What's Carla's story?" Sabre asked. She and Bob had just sat down to lunch at their newest Vietnamese restaurant, in search of the perfect #124, *bún thit nuóng*. When their favorite place, Pho Pasteur, closed, they'd had to find another. Bob had only eaten one thing on the menu, a fried pork and noodle dish, and they were determined to find another restaurant that measured up to the original.

"You spoke to her," Bob said. "Did she tell you anything?"

"Just that CPS has taken her daughter. She wanted me to represent her. I told her I couldn't, but that she has the best attorney here."

"Thank you, Sobs."

"You can call me if she needs calming down. That's what I was best at with her."

"Carla's a hoot," Bob said. "This will be an interesting case. She tried to take her own life, but she probably wasn't serious. She attempted to overdose on cough syrup, which actually can work. From what I understand, it can also make you hallucinate." Bob smirked. "She definitely doesn't need any help with that. She's already a little off center."

"But you *can* overdose on cough syrup, right?" Sabre looked up as the food server dropped off menus.

"People have. Mostly teenagers who discovered they can get a cheap high with it."

"That's a random thing to know."

"I read a lot on the internet. It's not that uncommon among teenage suicide attempts. But, according to the report, it made Carla sick to her stomach, so she threw up a lot. That's probably what saved her."

Bob opened his menu and found *bún thit nuóng*. They both ordered it.

"So, is Carla married?" Sabre asked.

"No."

"Who's the father?"

"She won't say. The girl is four years old. She was born on the fourth of July, so Carla named her Liberty. Can you imagine if she'd been born on Groundhog Day?"

Sabre chuckled. "You think she knows, and she's just not telling?"

"She knows. Or at least she claims to. Carla has nothing but good things to say about the father, except that he dumped her."

"After he found out she was pregnant?"

"I don't think she ever told him, but I'm not sure. She's sketchy about the details."

"Do you think she'll ever be able to parent the child properly, considering her history?"

"I don't know, but I'll fight for her rights just the same. That's my job. Dave Casey is the County Counsel, and Chucas is representing Liberty, so we have competent attorneys who will do their jobs. Since Carla thinks the baby daddy is great, I wish she'd name him— because if she ever succeeds at one of her attempts, at least we would know."

"And maybe he wants to be a father and would give that little girl a good home." Sabre paused while their food was delivered. "What about her mother? I never met her, but Ron seemed to like her."

"She's not in good health. Carla does have an older sister, Emma Griffin, who may be a possibility, but she and her husband are traveling right now and won't be home until tomorrow. They would've been here sooner, but by the time child services reached them, it was too late to get an earlier flight. The court ordered a home eval when the sister returns and discretion to detain with her."

"I don't think I ever met her."

"According to Carla, Emma is happily married to a man named Roger. They live locally, both are teachers, and they couldn't have children of their own, so they've helped raise Liberty."

"Do you have anything on calendar this afternoon?" Sabre asked.

"No. But I thought I'd hang around and watch your Harn/Stadler hearing if it doesn't take too long."

They continued with small talk while they ate their meals. On their way out of the restaurant, Sabre asked, "What did you think of the food?"

"I think we need to find another restaurant."

Chapter 5

Chapter 5

Monday afternoon

Before the hearing was called to order, the judge looked from Stadler to Harn. Then he directed his attention at Sabre's client and said, "Mr. Harn, I know you have feelings of rage over the allegations. Any good father would. However, you will not act out those feelings in my courtroom. And if you want custody of your child, you'll have to convince this court that you can control your anger." Judge Thomas softened his tone. "I need to know that your child is safe at home when no one is around to direct you. I know there has never been any indication that you have lost your temper with either your daughter or her mother. From all the evidence I have before me, which granted is very little, you have never been prone to violence. This is not the time to start. Do you understand me?"

"I do, Your Honor, and I sincerely apologize for my behavior. It was totally inappropriate and I assure you it will never happen again in, or outside, of your courtroom. My daughter is the most precious thing in my life, and I feel like I've failed to protect her." Grady choked up a little. "That's on me. But from here on out, I will do whatever the court orders to remedy that."

Judge Thomas turned to the defendant. "Wipe that silly look off your face."

Stadler sat up straighter and tried to appear expressionless.

"I don't know if you have a nervous twitch or if you're just arrogant, but that look on your face when the allegations were read this morning, and just now when I was talking to Mr. Harn, was disrespectful. I can understand why that set him off. Don't get me wrong, I do not in any way condone physical violence, and I will not tolerate it in my courtroom. I'll give you the benefit of the doubt today, but if that is a nervous habit, learn to control it. If it's purposeful, you need to change your attitude. Do you understand?"

"Your Honor," Attorney Blake cut in before his client could answer. "May I please speak to that?"

"No. You may not. We are not on the record, so you don't have to try to make one. But if you want it on the record, and I'm guessing you don't, I will gladly comply."

"No, Your Honor," Blake said, probably realizing it would be of no benefit to his client.

"Now, please answer my question, Mr. Stadler. Do you understand what I was telling you?"

"Yes, I do." A second later, he added. "Your Honor."

"Now, let's go on the record."

Stadler entered a denial to the petition and they set a trial date. The mother's attorney joined the father in a trial set.

Sabre stood. "Your Honor, I realize my client's behavior was less than stellar this morning, but he's a non-offending parent who has never hurt or neglected his child. I ask that the court detain Dakota with her father. I believe it's best for both him and the child. Her life has been totally disrupted and it might help give it some normalcy." Sabre glanced at her notes. "According to the report, Dakota wants not only to spend time with her father, but to live with him as well. Prior to this, she was in his home nearly half the time. A few years ago, when Dakota started kindergarten, he bought a house closer to her mother so Dakota could be with him and still attend the same school. If the court is not inclined to detain her there, then I would, in the alternative, ask for unsupervised visits."

The judge turned to County Counsel. "You were recommending detention with the father. Is that still your position?"

"We do not object to unsupervised visits," he said. "As for detention with the father, we'd like a little time to assess everything."

The judge didn't respond right away. He seemed to be struggling with his order. Finally, he said, "Mr. Harn, you do appear to be very devoted to your daughter, but I'm still concerned about your actions today. I won't detain Dakota with you this afternoon. However, I will allow liberal supervised visits. The social worker can lift the supervision if she chooses. I'm also ordering you into an anger management program. Once you have started the classes, I'll give discretion to the social worker, in conjunction with minor's attorney, to detain Dakota with you."

Attorney Blake argued for open supervised visits for Stadler and his biological daughter, Farrah, but said nothing about Dakota. The mother's attorney argued for unsupervised visitation with both her daughters.

The judge spoke to the defendant. "Mr. Stadler, you may have supervised visits with Farrah, and the supervisor will be determined by the social worker. It will not be the mother, and you will not have any contact with Dakota."

"Thank you, Your Honor," Blake said.

The judge turned to Mrs. Stadler. "You can have supervised visits with both of your daughters. The social worker has the discretion to lift the supervision on Farrah, but you are not allowed to let either of your girls around Mr. Stadler."

Her attorney made an argument for unsupervised visits, but it fell on deaf ears.

The judge looked directly at the mother. "I do not trust that you will keep your husband from either of your daughters. I understand that you want to believe him, and that at this point they are just allegations, but it's my job to protect this child, and until we have more definite answers, my orders will stand. You are not to be the supervisor for his visits with Farrah. Is that understood?"

"Understood, Your Honor," the mother's attorney said.

"Thank you, Counselor, but I'd like to hear that from your client."

The attorney whispered in the mother's ear, and she said meekly, "I understand."

When the hearing concluded, Sabre told her client she'd be in touch and walked out with Bob.

"I was hoping to see more fireworks," Bob said. "But it was fun hearing Judge Thomas chew out those men, especially Stadler."

"Most judges would want to say those things, but only Thomas would actually do it."

Chapter 6

Chapter 6

Monday evening

Sabre kicked off her shoes and plopped down on the sofa. She wanted a glass of wine, but she didn't have the energy to get one.

"You look like you were pulled through a knothole backward." JP, her live-in boyfriend and part-time investigator leaned down and kissed her cheek. "Rough day, baby?"

"Yeah. And I have a new case for you."

"Good. I'm not too busy right now. What is it?"

"Your favorite—a molestation by the stepfather." Sabre watched JP's handsome face flush with anger. Two things he hated most were child molesters and women beaters. "I represent the father, and it looks like it might go to trial. Stepfather denies everything, so right now it's the girl's word against his."

"How old is she?"

"Eight."

"Credible?"

"I believe so."

"What do you need me to do?"

"See if you can find any history. Old relationships that might give us something. The father wants custody."

"And the mother? Where does she stand?"

"Right now, she's supporting her husband. But up until this happened, she and my client had a good working relationship with shared custody."

"I'll get on it," JP said. "Can I get you a glass of wine?"

"You read my mind; I'd really appreciate that. I just need to sit for a minute and breathe."

Sabre watched as he walked to the kitchen, admiring his tall, buff body. When he returned with a glass of white wine, she asked, "Where are the kids?"

"Morgan and Dené are with Travis. Dené is starting to open up to her father, but she still feels more comfortable having Morgan with her. They're roller skating, of all things. Conner is biking with a friend. They should all be home within the hour."

"It's good to see Morgan and Dené doing things together. They may make it yet."

"They seem to get closer every day. Then there's those days when they can't seem to stand each other."

Morgan and Conner were JP's niece and nephew, his brother's kids. Their parents were both in prison. Gene would be released within the next few months, but their mother was serving twenty-five to life for murder. Sabre and JP had taken them in several months earlier. Shortly after that, their family grew again. Dené was Sabre's second cousin and had come to live with them just a month ago. Her father, Travis, had discovered he had a twelve-year-old daughter when Dené's mother passed away. The court and the family had decided Dené would be better off with Sabre until the girl and her father got to know each other. The process was moving slowly, but progress had been made.

Sabre headed to the kitchen to start dinner. She set down her glass of wine on the counter and began looking through the cupboards for something to make. The kids would be hungry when they got home, and it was her turn to cook. She set a large pan with water on the stove.

JP entered the kitchen. "If you're too tired, I can make dinner tonight."

"Thank you, but I'm fine. I'm making spaghetti and it's easy." She really didn't like to cook, but JP did it most of the time, and she wanted to do her share. She stopped what she was doing and looked at JP's sweet face.

"What?" he said in his Texas drawl.

"I'm just so happy to have you."

"I love you too."

"That's not what I said."

"But it's what you meant."

"Get out of here. I have a dinner to make."

~~~

JP was thinking about what Sabre had just said. She hadn't actually ever told him that she loved him, but he was confident that she did. Maybe confident wasn't quite the way he felt, but he knew she cared. He also knew she had difficulty expressing her feelings and he was willing to wait. Even if she wasn't quite where he was, he was willing to accept whatever she had to give. Conner was the first to return home, and interrupted his thoughts. "What's for dinner?"

"Spaghetti," JP said.

"Is Sabre making it?"

"Yes, why?"

"Because she makes it better than you do."

JP tousled his hair. "I may be getting old, but I can still take you."

Conner laughed. "That's why I keep working out, Uncle Johnny. One of these days." He walked into the kitchen. "Can I help with anything?"

"Only if you want garlic bread with the spaghetti," Sabre said.

"Yeah, I love that."
~~~

"Well, we don't have any. Would you mind driving to the store and picking up a loaf of French bread? You can take my car."

"Absolutely." Conner picked up her keys and hurried out the door. A moment later, he stepped back inside, JP handed him a twenty, and off he went.

Ten minutes later, Sabre heard the front door open, and Morgan walked in followed by Dené and Travis.

"How was the roller skating?" JP asked.

Sabre joined them in the living room. "Did you have fun?"

"It was great." Morgan spoke first and chattered on as usual. "Travis can really skate well, and so can Dené. They taught me a lot. I do okay, but they can both do lots of cool stuff on the skates. We went to Pacific Beach and skated along the Boardwalk. It's not very busy now because most of the tourists have gone home. Travis says it's too crowded in the summer, but it was perfect today. And it wasn't too hot. There were still enough people there, but not too many. And we saw this really old guy on roller skates. He was moving really slow and had his arms out like he was flying or something."

"Slow Mo," JP and Sabre said in unison.

"That's what Travis called him. Does everyone know him?"

"He's a legend," JP said. "He's been around for many, many years. Rumor has it he's a retired surgeon, but I don't know if it's true."

Sabre pivoted to Dené. "Did you have fun?"

"Yeah." She was a girl of few words, in complete contrast to Morgan who never seemed to stop chattering.

"I'm hungry. Is dinner ready?" Morgan asked. Before Sabre could answer, the girl continued. "Travis offered to stop and get something, but I texted Conner and he said you were making spaghetti, so we wanted to come home to eat."

"You chose my spaghetti over eating out?"

"It's the only thing you ma---ke really good." Morgan stopped; her mouth wide open. "I mean, it's the best thing you make."

But it was too late, and everyone was laughing, even Sabre.

"I'm sorry. I didn't mean that."

"Yes, you did. And it's fine. You're right. I'm not much of a cook. I'm just glad I make something everyone seems to like."

Morgan walked over to Sabre and led her to the kitchen. "Can I talk to you for a minute?"

Sabre thought she was going to apologize again, but instead Morgan whispered, "Can Travis stay for dinner?"

"Do you think Dené would be okay with that? I don't want to force him on her."

"She wants him to stay. She asked me to ask you."

"Of course. Text your brother and tell him to get two loaves of bread."

When Sabre asked Travis to stay for dinner, he glanced at Dené before responding. When she smiled, he said, "I'd love to. Thanks."

"Would you like a beer?" JP asked.

"That sounds great."

JP and Travis went out to the back porch, and Conner returned shortly with the bread.

"Girls, will you set the table for six please? And Conner, you can help me butter the bread."

Just as they all sat down to eat, the doorbell rang.

"I'll get it." Sabre got up.

"I hope you made enough spaghetti," Morgan said. "Whoever that is will probably want to eat too. It's probably some neighbor who smelled you cooking and came over just in time to eat."

Morgan was still babbling when Sabre opened the door and saw Bob standing there. Before she could invite him in, he blurted out, "Carla named the father of her baby, and you'll never guess who it is."

Chapter 7

Chapter 7

Monday night

Sabre tossed and turned in bed trying to get to sleep. She kept thinking about Carla naming Ron as the father. *It just couldn't be.* When she finally fell asleep she found herself in a dark room. In the distance, she heard the sad sound of a baby crying. She walked toward the cries and suddenly found herself standing in front of a drab courtroom. Judge Hekman was on the bench, and she doesn't look happy.

Sabre felt a sense of dread building up within her, and she struggled to hold back tears, though she didn't know why. Looking down, she noticed a small infant wrapped in a blanket lying on the hard, cold floor. The baby cried harder and Sabre feels the weight of the guilt weighing heavily on her chest. Slowly walking toward the infant, she picked it up with trembling hands. At that moment, Sabre noticed Ron standing in front of the judge with a somber expression on his face. She joined him.

"What's going on?" Sabre asked. "Why are you here?"

"That's my child," Ron said. "A petition has been filed on my newborn baby. They want to take jurisdiction and keep her in the juvenile dependency system."

"What are the allegations?" Sabre asked.

Ron couldn't speak. He was too upset and confused.

"Neglect," the judge said. "Please let us continue."

Sabre was shocked. "What are the specifics of the allegations? What is it he supposedly did to neglect his child?"

"He let her live with a crazy woman. He didn't step forward and claim her."

"I didn't know about her," Ron protested.

"You need to leave, Ms. Brown," the judge said. Then she turned to Ron and scolded him like a small boy.

Sabre felt helpless as she watched the judge yell at her brother. Then the judge announced the rulings.

"Please help me, Sabre," Ron pleaded. "Help me save my child."

"You said last night that this wasn't your child."

"But what if it is?"

"Well, is it, or not?"

"No. Yes. I don't know."

"It's beyond my control," Sabre said.

The baby continued to cry as Sabre stepped back and bowed her head in silence, feeling the weight of her failure. Sabre fell to her knees beside the crying infant, still gripping the now silent child in despair. She watched as the bailiff handcuffed Ron and took him away.

"Ron! Come back! Let him go," she shouted.

"Sabre, wake up," JP said, gently shaking her. She sat up abruptly. "Are you okay?" he asked.

Tears ran down Sabre's cheeks. She glanced around the room. "Where's Ron?"

"He's not here. You were having a nightmare."

She took a deep breath and blew it out, trying to clear her head. She finally realized where she was. "I'm sorry."

"What were you dreaming about?"

"Judge Hekman was very angry."

"Do you have a case in front of Hekman coming up? Is that what's bothering you?"

"I always have cases in her court, but this one was about Ron and his baby."

Tuesday morning

"Ron cannot be the father of Carla's baby," Sabre said harshly as she and Bob sat in a courthouse hall, waiting for a hearing. "It's not possible."

"Don't kill the messenger. I'm just telling you what my client said."

Sabre took a deep breath and lowered her voice. "Ron hasn't had any contact with her since before he went into witness protection. He's been back for almost two years now, but he was gone for five. The kid is four years old. It doesn't add up."

"I know." Bob smiled. "I don't really believe she's Ron's either. Carla says a lot of wacky things, but I think it's hilarious."

"Of course, you would."

"How is Ron reacting to it?"

"He's not concerned because he says there is no way he could be the father." Sabre had called her brother right after Bob had stopped by with the news.

"Is he willing to take a paternity test?"

"He has no qualms about it. In fact, he'd like to get it done right away, and get this ridiculous notion over with. He asked me to represent him if needed to get through the process. I told him that wasn't necessary. If you could give me the name and number of the social worker, Ron can call and voluntarily take the test."

"It's that cute little Laurie Snider. She's easy to work with and has a good sense of humor." Bob cocked his head. "Do you know her?"

"I had her on a case a few months ago. She was good."

"I don't have her number on me, but give me one second and I'll call the office and get it."

"Thanks, you're a sweetheart." *Despite his occasional sexist comments.*

Bob made a call and repeated the number out loud. Sabre entered it into her phone, along with the name Laurie Snider. Then she called Ron and gave him the information.

"It's all set. He can handle it from here."

Bob smirked.

"What are you grinning about?"

"He can handle it—unless he's the father."

"He's not. Ron hasn't seen her in years, so unless Liberty is twice as old as the mother says she is, he has nothing to worry about."

"That's it. Maybe the girl has Highlander Syndrome."

"What's that?"

"It's a genetic mutation that keeps a child from developing into an adult. They always look younger than they are. So, maybe she's really eight or nine, not four."

"How do you know this stuff?" Sabre shook her head. "That's not possible anyway. The court knows when the child was born."

"I know. I'm just messing with you. If Ron says he's not the father, I'm sure he's not. Who knows? Next, she might say it's Elvis."

"Maybe it is. He's still alive, you know." Sabre laughed.

Bob ignored her. "I can't imagine what it would be like to share a child with Crazy Carla."

Sabre frowned at him for his insensitivity, but there was no point in saying anything. Bob was never going to change, and she knew he was actually a very compassionate man. Most of his inappropriate comments were intended just to annoy her.

Chapter 8

Chapter 8

Tuesday morning

JP sat at his desk at home perusing the Harn/Stadler case. His blood pressure elevated when he read the report. Dakota was very clear on her allegations of molestation, and it sounded like a classic case of grooming.

She reported that Stadler hugged her a lot, which she didn't mind at first, except that he would hold on a little too long. When he said goodnight, he had kissed her on the lips. At first, it was just a quick kiss, but that also started to linger. She hadn't told her mother because her mother seemed so happy and Stadler was good to them in so many ways. He worked a lot and wasn't around most of the day. On the weekends, when Dakota wasn't with her father, they would go places and do things as a family, and Stadler had always been appropriate on their outings.

Then he'd started giving her backrubs at night when she went to bed, raising her pajama top to massage her bare skin. After a few months, he'd started touching other parts of her body. The first time, she'd jumped up, ran to the bathroom and threw up. Stadler had checked on her, then left.

JP flung the report and slammed his fist on the desk. He hated even reading this stuff. His first impulse was to go remove the scumbag from the earth.

To calm himself, JP went outside for some fresh air. Louie, his beagle, ran to him with a stick, wanting to play fetch. JP threw the stick across the yard. Within seconds, Louie brought it back, and he threw it again. After about five minutes, JP stopped. He knew Louie would never call the game if he didn't. The dog tried several times to entice him into throwing it again but finally gave up and rubbed against JP's leg affectionately. JP bent down and scratched the dog's head and behind his ears.

"Too bad people aren't as nice as animals," JP said. "This would be a much better world. You're a good dog, Louie."

He went back inside and continued reading the report. Dakota had tried telling her mother, but her mom had been busy with the baby and tired all the time. Dakota never told her father because she was afraid of what he might do. Stadler had planted many seeds in her brain about not sharing their "little secret" with her mother or father. Once he'd said, "You wouldn't want your father to go to jail, would you? You know he'd be jealous of what we have, and he would probably try to kill me."

JP could barely contain himself, feeling his face flush with heat. He didn't blame Harn one bit for attacking Stadler in court. He would've done much more than that.

Child Protective Services had already run a criminal check on Stadler and found nothing significant, but JP ran another, just in case. He came up empty as well. He checked out Stadler's social media accounts, but they were mostly LinkedIn business postings. The perv didn't seem to be on Twitter, Instagram, or TikTok. He did have a Facebook page, but again, he mostly posted business stuff.

JP searched for background information and found that Stadler had been born and raised in La Jolla. His parents were both attorneys, and based on his high school online yearbook, Stadler had not been part of the *in crowd*. His grades had been very good, but he wasn't at the top of his class. Stadler hadn't held any class offices, but he'd joined several voluntary groups. He appeared to have been right on the edge of things, but never quite in the mix. Stadler was also a big model train enthusiast, which JP found curious. As a kid, he'd always been fascinated with trains himself. JP shuddered. He didn't like the thought of sharing any interest with this scumbag.

He continued to search the internet until he had enough information to hit the streets. Except for Stadler's time at the University of Arizona, the man had lived his entire life in La Jolla, so JP figured finding people who knew him well would be easy. He had a list and had already set up a couple of appointments with Stadler's co-workers. The first was at noon. In the meantime, JP would check his neighborhood. Stadler was still living in the home he'd grown up in, which he'd inherited. Other than the dorm in Arizona, it was the only residential address on record for him.

JP drove to Stadler's home in La Jolla. The property was impressive, sitting on the side of a hill with a view of the ocean. Lots of houses were crowded on the hill next to it, but this one stood out from the rest. It was twice the size of most of the others and on a corner lot with the best view.

JP parked a couple houses down from Stadler's, got out of the truck, and started knocking on doors. The first house, no one answered. The next one, the residents had only lived there a few months and didn't know the Stadlers or anyone else in the neighborhood. At the third house, the smallest on the block, a woman in her fifties answered the door. JP explained that he was an investigator, but that he couldn't disclose any details of the case. She seemed to be fine with that.

"Who is it, honey?" a man asked, walking up behind the woman.

"It's an investigator. He wants to ask us some questions about a neighbor."

"Which neighbor?" the man asked JP.

"Ritchie Stadler."

"It figures. Come on in."

JP reached out his hand. "I'm JP Torn, private investigator."

The man reciprocated. "Evan Green, San Diego Deputy Sheriff." He introduced his wife, Anne.

"Nice to meet you. I'm retired law enforcement, San Diego PD."

"Good to meet you as well, brother. Have a seat. What can we do for you?"

They all sat in a tidy living room filled with decorative vases. "How long have you lived here?"

"Twenty-one years."

"Did you know Stadler's parents?"

"No. Ritchie was living there alone when we moved in. He's not very friendly, or maybe just private, but he keeps to himself."

"Do you know his wife?"

"I've spoken to Heidi a few times. She moved in a few years ago. My wife knows her better." He turned to Anne.

"I like her a lot," she said. "I don't know her well, but she seems to be a good mother. Dakota is a sweetheart and so is the little one, Farrah."

"Have you been inside their house?" JP asked.

"A few times."

"Have you ever seen Stadler with the girls?"

The man's expression turned solemn, and before his wife could answer, Green said, "If this is a juvenile court case—and I know you can't reveal that—we'll help in any way we can."

"Understood." JP relaxed a little with his questions. Green knew exactly what he was looking for. It was a lot easier asking questions he didn't have to skirt around. "Have either of you seen Stadler with the girls?"

"He works a lot," Anne said, "but he takes care of the girls when Heidi runs errands and such. Dakota spends a lot of time with her real father."

"I'm curious," JP said looking at Green. "When I told you it was Stadler I was investigating, why did you respond the way you did?"

"Nothing substantial, but I find him a little off-putting. I've done a little investigating on him myself, and his business practices are shaky. Nothing criminal, but he seems to be right on the edge. More importantly, you might be interested in the families he had living with him over the years."

JP felt the hairs on his neck stand at attention. "Tell me about them."

"The first one I knew of was about eight or nine years ago. The woman was there quite a while, but I couldn't tell you exactly how long. I really don't remember much about her, or her child."

"She had a little girl about five years old," Anne chimed in. "But we didn't see her much."

"The last one was about a year before he got married," Evan said. "He was dating a woman who had a daughter about six or seven. She moved in, but only stayed a few months. Frankly, I didn't like the way he looked at the girl or acted around her."

"Like what?"

"He was always carrying her around, holding her real close. He seemed more interested in the little girl than he did the mother. I realize he could just love children, but his behavior gave me a bad vibe."

Knowing what he knew, the details turned JP's stomach. "That fits."

"I may be way off base because I don't really have any evidence of wrongdoing, but I've spent a lot of time working special victims. I may be oversensitive, so do with it what you will."

"Do you know the woman's name who lived there last? Or how to contact her?"

"No." Evan turned to his wife. "Do you remember, Anne?"

"I'm trying to think. It was Melanie, or Marian, or Mandy. I can't remember, but I think it started with an M."

"I appreciate the info. You've been a big help."

"Have you talked to their next-door neighbor, Thelma Carter?" Anne asked. "She lives two doors north from us. She's old, but she's sharp and has lived there for over sixty years. She could probably tell you a lot more than we can."

"I stopped by, but no one answered."

"Today is her bridge day, but if you try her tomorrow around eleven, you'll probably catch her at home."

"Thanks, I will."

JP knocked on a few more doors, but didn't find anyone at home. He checked his watch. He had enough time to get to his appointment. He was meeting a woman for lunch who'd worked with Stadler a few years ago, but had moved to another company after a huge disagreement with Stadler, who'd been her supervisor.

He hoped he wouldn't be wasting his time. He realized talking to Stadler's co-workers wasn't likely to produce information he needed for the juvenile case. He decided he wouldn't spend much more time on Stadler's business dealings, but in case the creep didn't get charged with the molestation, maybe he would at least go down on some kind of fraud charge.

Chapter 9

Chapter 9

Tuesday noon

JP walked into the sandwich shop and looked around for a tall woman wearing a red blouse, as she'd described herself. She wasn't there, so he ordered a pastrami sandwich. As he paid for the meal, a tall, dark-haired woman in her mid- to late-twenties walked in the door. She wore a sleek black skirt and a bright red blouse.

JP stepped toward her. "Are you Stacy?"

She nodded.

"I'm JP Torn."

"Nice to meet you."

"Can I get your lunch?"

"I ordered ahead and paid for it, but thank you."

They picked up their sandwiches, and Stacy suggested they sit outside. JP followed her to an empty table. It was a little noisy from the vehicles, but a beautiful sunny day.

"You wanted to talk about Ritchie Stadler?" she asked. Then took a bite of her sandwich.

JP liked that she got right to the point. "Yes. How long did you work with him?"

"For about a year. It was my first job in the financial field, so I was pretty raw. Ritchie was my immediate supervisor. I was uncomfortable right from the beginning about the way he did things, but I thought maybe I just didn't know the ropes.

God knows, he told me that plenty of times. I thought maybe I was just in the wrong business, that everyone worked that way. It took me a while to realize it was just him."

"What exactly did he do?"

"That's the problem. I could never quite put my finger on it. But he seemed to really take advantage of the elderly. He took risks that made him money, but didn't always benefit his clients. He was quite successful, so the company backed him."

"Did you complain about him?"

"I did, but it didn't get me anywhere. Then he made my life very uncomfortable."

"Did he threaten you or hurt you?"

"No." Stacy shook her head. "He just gave me terrible clients. He made it impossible for me to be successful, then wrote bad reviews on me. He was too much of a coward to actually confront me or deal above board. Then something happened that really got me scared, so I left."

"What happened?"

"He had an older client named Uri Moss who was looking for a place to invest his money. He was a retired flight instructor for a small airport, so he didn't have a lot of money. Besides his home, he only had about four hundred thousand dollars, but it was his life savings. Stadler persuaded him to do a reverse mortgage and invest another five hundred and ninety thousand with him in a *sure thing*." She rolled her eyes at the thought. "Stadler claimed it would pay off ninety to a hundred grand a year, so he and his wife could live comfortably and travel. Uri was reluctant, and the wife even more so, but Stadler convinced them both."

JP knew where this was going. "And the investment didn't pan out?"

"A total loss, but Stadler still got his commissions. Granted, he would've done better if it had been a win, but either way, he stood to make big money on the deal. Uri was irate and totally flipped out."

"What did he do?"

A car honked as another car abruptly pulled in front of him. Brakes screeched. Other cars maneuvered out of the way. Stacy sat back suddenly as if the car was coming her way, then chuckled at her foolish move. "That startled me," she said. "Where was I?"

"You were talking about Uri Moss."

"That's right." She took a deep breath. "He came into the office and held us at gunpoint. I was so scared, but Stadler was worse. I thought he was going to pee his pants. Security came in, and Uri backed right down. He apologized for scaring me, but he told Stadler he wasn't done with him."

"Was Uri arrested?"

"No. Stadler didn't want to press charges, and the company didn't want the scandal."

"I can see why that was your final straw."

"I would've quit the whole business, but a friend convinced me that not all companies were like that. He put in a good word for me with his employer, and I got the job. I love it there." She continued to eat.

"As far as you know, has Stadler had any formal complaints about his work?"

"There's been a few investigations because of money people lost, but none were ever considered fraud or anything. It's not like he embezzles money. If he did that, he'd surely get caught. He just pressures people to invest their money where they often shouldn't, then makes bank even if they lose."

"If he's losing money for people, why do they keep him around?"

"Because more often, he makes money. Stadler's very lucky. When it works, it works big. The client makes money and so does the company. He's an excellent salesman. He has the gift of gab. He has persuaded more than one elderly person to take a reverse mortgage on their home and invest the money with him."

"Is that illegal?"

"Not really. But it's not always in their best interest. Like I said, it would be hard to make a case against him, but his reputation is starting to spiral. Hopefully, it'll catch up to him soon."

"Do you know anything about his personal life?"

"I never saw him outside of work. I know he got married just as I was leaving the company, but as you can imagine, I wasn't invited to the wedding." Stacy gave a sardonic smile, then finished her sandwich. "I need to go," she said as she stood.

"Thanks." JP stood too, a respectful habit. "I appreciate your time."

As he finished eating, his second interview walked up. The man still worked with Stadler, and it was evident he didn't like Ritchie, but he also didn't have any real information to provide. He had been invited to the wedding, but chose not to go. JP wondered if anyone had shown for the event.

Chapter 10

Chapter 10

Wednesday morning

At eleven sharp, JP knocked on the door next to Stadler's house. A spry, elderly woman answered. JP was sure she didn't reach five feet and weighed less than a hundred pounds.

"Thelma Carter?"

"I'm Thelma."

"My name is JP Torn. I'm a private investigator, and I'd like to ask you some questions about your neighbors."

"You must be that nice young man Anne mentioned. She spoke highly of you." She stepped back and opened the door wide. "Do come in. I don't know what good talking to me will do, but I'll help if I can. And if I can't, I'm sure I'll enjoy the company, so at least one of us will benefit."

JP liked her wit. "Thank you, ma'am. I appreciate it." He followed her inside.

"Have a seat anywhere."

The room was filled with dark furniture, and the shades were drawn, making it a little gloomy. JP sat in the over-stuffed chair that was worn with age, but still comfortable.

"I'm sorry it's so dark in here. Bright lights sometimes hurt my head."

"It's fine."

"Can I get you some tea or coffee?" She hovered nearby.

"No, thank you."

"Water?"

"I'm good."

"How about a soft drink? I have Pepsi, Coke, Sprite, and Dr. Pepper."

JP felt like he'd better take something or she'd keep asking until he did. "I'll have a Pepsi."

She scurried out of the room like a squirrel in search of a nut. She was surprisingly quick for her age. JP walked over to the fireplace to look at the photos on the mantel. There were some with kids, graduation photos, wedding photos, and several with Thelma and a ruggedly handsome man. JP wondered if he was her husband. He sat back down before she returned.

She came in carrying a can of Pepsi and handed it to him. "It's cold. I would've brought a glass with ice, but you strike me as a 'drink straight from the can' kind of guy. But if I'm wrong, I'll bring you a glass."

"You're not wrong." JP liked her even more.

Thelma sat on the sofa closest to JP's chair. She curled up with her legs underneath her like a little girl. "Now, what can I do for you?"

"I hear you've lived in the neighborhood awhile. How long exactly?"

"It'll be sixty-six years next month. I moved here when I was twenty-three, a year after we got married. My husband and I bought the house for thirty-four thousand, five hundred dollars. We weren't sure if we could make the payments, nearly a hundred dollars a month. It took two teaching salaries and a tight budget, but somehow we managed." She laughed. "Today, they tell me it's worth millions. I can't even fathom that. My grandkids say I should sell it and 'live the life.' What they don't understand is that I've already lived the life I wanted. I'm perfectly happy. The only thing that would be better is if my husband would've lived to enjoy our retirement years. He's been gone almost twenty years. Cancer got him."

"I'm sorry to hear that."

"It's okay. I stopped grieving a long time ago. Now, I just remember the good times. And there were so many." Her eyes lit up with memories. "Like time with our daughter when she was young and all of us watching the sunsets on the beach. And waltzing. I'll never forget the dances. The present is great too. My daughter, my grandkids, and my great-grandkids spend a lot of time with me. Plus, I have my bridge friends. It's a good life." She smiled. "But you didn't come here to talk about my personal life. What neighbors would you like the skinny on?"

JP took a notebook and pen out of his pocket. "Do you mind if I take notes? The memory isn't what it used to be."

"Go ahead. I know exactly what you mean. Lots of things I can't remember that I used to."

JP jotted down a few details to establish a timeline. "How well do you know the Stadlers?"

"I knew Frank and Gladys really well. I felt bad for Gladys when Frank left her for a young law clerk. He had a roving eye, that one. But she always trusted him, poor thing. It's a wonder they made it as long as they did. They both worked so much. They hardly saw one another. Gladys was heartbroken, but she had a son to raise, so she cowgirled up and did whatever she had to do."

"How old was Ritchie when his father left?"

"About eight."

JP's phone buzzed in his pocket. He took it out and declined the call.

"You can answer that if you'd like."

"It can wait." He stuck the phone back in his shirt pocket. "Ritchie's mother never remarried?"

"She dated some, but there was never anyone serious that I knew of. She confided in me quite a bit. She didn't seem to have other gal pals. She worked and doted on her son. That's about all. She wanted to learn to play bridge, so I taught her."

"Does she live with the Stadlers now?"

"Oh no. She passed away some years ago. Ritchie was in his early twenties, not long after he moved back from Arizona, maybe a year after he graduated from college." A long-haired rag-doll cat jumped up on her lap, and she began to pet him. "His mother had already been diagnosed with ovarian cancer but she kept it from him until she got too sick. To his credit, he took good care of his mother right up until she passed, and she was pretty ill at the end."

"That's a beautiful cat. What's his name?"

"Camden. He's my buddy. I've only had him a little over a year. I don't know what I'd do without him."

"Animals become part of the family." JP could hear Camden's loud purr as he continued. "After his mother died, did Ritchie live there alone until he married?"

Thelma smiled and shook her head. "He only lived alone for about a year, then Belle and her daughter moved in. She stayed a year, then moved out. I really liked that little girl. She was so bubbly and full of life. She loved to come over and play in my backyard."

JP did the math in his head. Belle couldn't have been one of the women the Greens mentioned because she would've been before their time. So, there were at least three women with small daughters prior to Heidi and Dakota. Stadler certainly had a pattern. JP had to wonder why he'd married Heidi, and perhaps more importantly, why the others hadn't lasted long.

"How well did you know Belle?"

"Not well, other than knowing she was quite young and very attractive. She had a pretty amazing body." She reflected. "I had a body like that once. Maybe not that nice, but I'm sure she paid extra for those breasts. That was never that important to me, or to my husband, so I kept what God gave me."

JP was starting to get used to her bluntness. "Do you know Belle's last name?"

"She just went by Belle. She said she dropped her last name for work."

"What kind of work?"

"She was a stripper at one of those bars near Rosecrans. She wasn't ashamed of it. In fact, she seemed quite proud of her work. I'm not sure that sat well with Ritchie. He was always a bit of a prude."

That's not the word he would've used for him. JP kept it to himself and asked, "Do you know what happened to their relationship?"

"They argued a lot. I could hear them sometimes. But I don't know what caused the split."

"Were there others after Belle?"

"There was Izzy." She thought for a minute. "Katherine and Melodi, but with an 'i'. In that order."

"Wow. You remember all their names and spellings." Camden jumped down, rubbed against JP's leg, but before he could pet him, he dashed off.

"Melodi had a thing about people spelling her name correctly," Thelma said. "That's the way she introduced herself. And I saw it on her name tag whenever she had her uniform on. I remember the women mostly because it was delightful having them here. That was because of the children more than anything. They all had little girls, and I enjoyed them immensely."

"No boys?"

"Nope, not a one."

At this point, that didn't surprise him. "Tell me about Izzy."

"She was the only one with dark hair, except for his wife. The others were all blondes, although I'm pretty sure Belle's wasn't natural. Not that it matters. I used to color my hair too, to cover the gray. Now I let it go white, and I kind of like it. I'm not fooling anyone with my age anymore."

"I don't know about that. You look and act a lot younger than you are."

"Well, thank you, Mr. Torn. That's the nicest thing anyone has said to me in a while." She sat up a little taller. "Back to Izzy. Her little girl's name was Natalie. I think she was four. That's right, because she had her fifth birthday when she was living there. I didn't see as much of Natalie as some of the others. She seemed a little slow. I think she had some issues."

"How long were they there?"

"About six months."

"Do you know what broke them up?"

"No idea."

Thelma's phone rang. It had been a long time since JP heard a landline ring. All they'd had in his home for a while now were cell phones.

"Would you please excuse me? It's probably my daughter, and she'll worry if I don't answer."

"No problem." JP stood. "I'll step outside and make a call myself."

Chapter 11

Chapter 11

JP went back into the house and sat in the same chair. "Is your daughter satisfied that you're okay?"

"Yeah. They're all worry warts, but she's the worst." Thelma leaned forward. "Now, where were we?"

"You said Katherine was next?"

"That's right. Katherine Jackson, a nice girl. She stayed quite a while, almost a year, I think."

"And she had a daughter as well?"

"Yes. Her name was Opal. I think she was six when they moved in. She'd come see me a lot. Sometimes she helped make cookies. I even babysat her from time to time. She was a sweet little girl, and Katherine was a delight. She spent a lot of time over here, drinking tea and just visiting."

"Do you know why Katherine left?"

"It was rather abrupt. She was here one afternoon and everything seemed fine, and the next day she moved out."

"Did she tell you she was leaving?"

"No. But she called me a few days later and said they just didn't see eye to eye, but I got the feeling it was more than that. That was eight or nine years ago, but she still keeps in touch. I get Christmas and birthday cards every year, and we talk on the phone about every six months or so."

"How's Opal doing?"

"She's great. She's fifteen now and gets good grades. I met Katherine and Opal for lunch one day a few months ago. Opal is a beautiful young girl."

"Would you mind giving me Katherine's contact information? I'd like to ask her a few questions."

"No problem. I'm sure she wouldn't mind."

Thelma walked over to a small desk in the corner of the room. She removed an address book and returned. She gave him the address and phone number for Katherine, then thumbed through the book again. "Izzy's last name was Hernandez."

"Do you have her contact info?"

"Just her name. I never heard from her after she left. The only one I kept in touch with was Katherine. Ritchie lived alone for about five years until he met Melodi, and that didn't last long. She was only there about three months."

"How old was Melodi's daughter?"

Thelma suddenly closed her eyes and pressed a hand to her forehead.

"Are you okay?"

She sat still for a moment without speaking. Her head bobbed a few times, then she blinked rapidly and said, "I'm fine. Just a little pain. It comes and goes. That's what happens when you get old."

"Have you been to a doctor?"

"I've been to many doctors. It's nothing to worry about."

JP kept an eye on her, concerned that the issue was more complex than she'd admitted. But within a few minutes, she was back to normal.

"Now, where were we?" Thelma asked again.

"You were telling me about Melodi. How old was her daughter when they lived with Stadler?"

"Paige was six or seven, a little older than the others. I don't think she liked Ritchie very much. Maybe that's why it didn't work for them."

"What makes you think she didn't like him?"

"She preferred to stay with me when her mother was working."

"How often did you watch her?"

"Paige was with me a half dozen times while Melodi worked part time at Marshalls. She tried to get day shifts, but she couldn't always manage it. Paige was a real pistol, not afraid to speak her mind. I didn't see a whole lot of either of them. First of all, they were only next door a very short time, and Paige stayed with her grandmother a lot, mostly on weekends."

"Did you ever meet her father?"

"No. He never came here. At least I never saw him. I'm pretty sure he was in prison or something, but Melodi never told me that. I only think that because of some things Paige said. She talked about him all the time. She was quite attached."

"Do you remember Melodi's last name?"

"I'm not sure I ever knew it. I didn't really get to know her well."

"But she trusted you with her child?"

"I have a good reputation in the neighborhood. I did day-care for a while after I retired from teaching. The kids always wanted to come here to play. I have a fun backyard, and the people in the Stadler house could see it from their second story. Come see." The old woman stood and started toward the back of the house. JP followed.

When they stepped outside, JP said, "Well, if that don't put pepper in your gumbo!" JP looked around, taking it all in—a huge tubular slide, a trampoline, a playhouse that looked like a castle, and monkey bars, all in bright colors. A big plastic pirate ship sat in the back of the huge yard. "This is amazing. It's a backyard playground. More like a mini-Disneyland. No wonder kids love to come here." JP walked out onto the green spongy flooring. "This is incredible."

"Thanks. It takes a lot of upkeep, but I don't have anything else to spend my money on. My great-grandkids love it too."

"I'm sure they do."

Thelma led him back inside. On the way, JP asked, "How well do you know Heidi?"

"Pretty well."

"Do you ever babysit Dakota or Farrah?"

"No. I'm getting too old for that. I can't keep up with the little ones like I used to. But Heidi brings the girls over once in a while to play in the backyard. Dakota is sweet and so is Farrah. I love having them, but I can't chase after the little ones anymore."

"You have been amazing. Thank you so much for the delightful conversation."

"It was my pleasure. You know, I wouldn't have invited you in, and I wouldn't have shared so much information if Anne hadn't told me to talk to you."

"Actually, that's good to know. You can't be too careful."

"I have one question, and if you can't answer it, I understand."

"Try me."

"I've known Ritchie Stadler all his life. He was a cute little boy, a bit odd as a teenager, and I don't think he has grown into an honest man. I've heard things about his business dealings that do not impress me. I don't think your investigation is about that, and I expect you probably can't tell me. I was a foster parent for years, so I know what goes on out there in the world. We took care of some lovely children. One of them we adopted."

"Good for you."

"Those kids have it pretty rough, but our daughter turned out well. She's a lovely woman now. She had some rocky patches, a bad marriage, but she finally changed all that. She's much happier now, and she loves her job. She works with children who are going through the same things she did before she came to us."

"I'm sure she turned out well because you offered her a safe home and lots of love. Not every child gets that."

"I know. I should've done more to help protect them."

"Protect who?"

"All the children in the world. Oh, I know I can't protect them all, but I missed a few opportunities to help kids when I should have."

"I'm sure you've helped more than you realize."

"Well, that's spilled milk now." For a second, she looked sad, then bubbled up again. "To get back to my question. From your line of inquiry, and the fact that some woman picked up Dakota and Farrah a few days ago, I've come to my own conclusions. Right or wrong, it doesn't really matter. I won't share them with anyone because they are only guesses and spreading them would create gossip, and I don't do that. So, for my question. Can *you* tell me what's going on?"

"I'm sorry. I can't, but I can assure you that the girls are both doing fine."

Thelma gave a quick smile. "Thank you."

Chapter 12

Chapter 12

Wednesday afternoon

JP looked at the list of people he wanted to interview; Belle, Izzy Hernandez, Katherine Jackson, and Melodi. He didn't have much hope of finding Belle. He had no last name, and it had been twenty years since she worked as a stripper in some bar near Rosecrans. She'd be in her forties now and chances are she had moved on. He would put Ron on that task. He'd have fun searching and was pretty good at that kind of legwork.

Izzy wasn't much of a prospect either. He put them both on the back burner and called Katherine. She was his best bet.

"Hello," a pleasant voice answered.

"Hi. My name is JP Torn. Is this Katherine Jackson?"

"Yes."

"Thelma gave me your phone number. She said you may be able to help me. I'm a private investigator, and I'm gathering information about Ritchie Stadler."

For a moment, the line was quiet. "I haven't seen him in almost ten years."

"I figured that, but I think you may be able to shed some light on a few things for us. Would you mind talking with me? We can meet anywhere you want." When she hesitated again, he said, "Why don't you call Thelma and talk to her? I think she'll assure you that this is important."

"I'll call her, and if you don't hear from me, then I'm out."

"Fair enough."

JP went back to his list. He wanted to talk to Melodi. Even though it had been approximately four years since she lived with him, she was the most recent. Also, she'd left abruptly, which might mean something happened that could affect this case. But how would he track her without a last name? All he really knew was her workplace from four or five years ago, but it was a start. He looked up the locations for local Marshalls stores. He found four in San Diego alone, and one each in La Jolla, Mira Mesa, Solana Beach, San Ysidro, El Cajon, and Chula Vista. Not to mention outlying cities. Melodi could be at any of them, or at none. He mapped them out to establish the shortest route and started his search.

His first stop was in La Jolla, the closest to where Stadler lived. When he walked in, he realized what a daunting task it would be. Most of the employees were in their early twenties, which meant they likely hadn't worked there long. That would be okay if Melodi was still an employee. He decided to start with someone a little older. He walked through the store until he found a clerk who appeared to be in her fifties. Her name tag read: ROBIN.

"Excuse me," JP said.

"May I help you with something?"

"Robin, is it?"

"Yes. What can I do for you?"

"Is there a woman working here named Melodi?"

"I don't think so."

"I know she worked at this store a few years ago," he said, embellishing a little, "but I'm not sure if she's still here or transferred somewhere."

"I'm sorry, but I just started working for Marshalls about six weeks ago. I haven't met anyone named Melodi, but that doesn't mean she isn't an employee. You could ask Joan. She's the store manager."

"Where would I find her?"

Robin nodded her head toward an employee. "She's the woman over there by the jewelry."

"Thanks." JP smiled and walked away.

He approached the woman Robin had pointed to. "Are you the store manager?"

"Yes. What can I help you with?"

"I'm looking for a Marshalls' employee named Melodi."

"What do you need her for?"

JP had thought of several cover stories that might work, but he decided the truth was the best approach. He could do that without disclosing any information about the case. "I'm a private investigator for a juvenile dependency case. It doesn't involve Melodi, but she may be able to help us protect two little girls who are in danger."

A look of concern crossed Joan's face. "I don't have anyone here now named Melodi. Do you know her last name?"

"Unfortunately, I do not. All I know is that she worked at Marshalls about four or five years ago. I'm not even certain it was this store."

"I've been here for seven years, and I don't remember a Melodi. But we've had dozens of employees come and go. Without a last name, she'd be difficult to locate."

JP gave her his card. "Please call if you remember anything."

"I'll do one better. I'll look through past records and see if I come across anyone with that name. I can't guarantee when I'll get it done though."

"I appreciate anything you can do."

JP had a similar experience at the next Marshalls store. He'd gone straight to the manager, who'd been no help. Then he'd walked around the store and spoken to a couple of employees, but got nowhere.

Back in his truck, JP felt frustrated and bored. He didn't enjoy this kind of investigating. Consequently, he was thrilled when his phone rang and it was Katherine. She agreed to meet him for coffee at Starbucks on Rosecrans in half an hour. JP called Ron to assist.

"Are you busy?"

"Right now, I'm on my way to get a paternity test. You know, the usual everyday stuff."

"That was a shocker when Bob told us."

"It's just Carla being Carla. I know I'm not the father. I was in Washington at the time the child was conceived. I just need to do this so maybe they can find the real father. I feel bad for Carla. Reality isn't her strong suit."

"You're a good man, Ron," JP said. "Want some work?"

"Sure. What is it?"

"The first one is boring, but I have another that will be far more interesting. You'll need to do that one at night. The job suits you." He explained about Melodi and gave him the information.

"That's the boring one, right?"

"Yep. The other one will require visits to strip clubs."

Ron laughed. "It's been a few years since I've done that, but anything for the job."

"Maybe you can get Bob to go with you. He's always entertaining in those situations."

"True enough." Ron laughed. "After my test, I have an appointment with Attorney Doyle. That shouldn't take long. Then I can get started on your job."

"Doyle is the attorney for the Silent Thunder Charity, right?"

"Yes. I need to become active with the company. It's been a couple of months since the Incognito Angel has struck." Ron and Sabre's aunt had recently passed away and left them a well-funded charity whose mission was to find deserving people and anonymously solve their immediate problem.

The gift could be big or small, but the point was to make a significant change in their lives. A reporter had dubbed her the *Incognito Angel*.

"How does it feel to make people's dreams come true?"

"I don't know. I haven't made any gifts yet."

"It sounds like fun." JP gave him what little he knew about Belle, then drove to his home so he could do a few things in his office before he met with Katherine.

Chapter 13

Chapter 13

Wednesday late afternoon

Ron sat in the waiting room listening for his name to be called for his DNA test. He was quite relaxed knowing that the test would be negative. He felt sorry for Carla. She was a beautiful woman with a kind heart and serious mental issues. He felt a little guilty for the part he'd played in her breakdown. He certainly hadn't done anything intentionally to hurt her, but he knew when he'd left it had been the final straw in her breakdown.

She had always loved him more than he'd loved her, but he still cared about her and would have stuck with her back then . . . if life hadn't gotten in the way. And it wasn't like he'd had a choice when he'd left. Taking her from her family and her stability would've been far worse. But she was obviously still stuck in the past, or she wouldn't have named him as the father. Ron sighed. He couldn't do much, but this was the best thing he could do for her. Proving he wasn't the father might help her start to get back to reality.

Once he was called, it didn't take long to do the test. He was out of there within twenty minutes and on his way to Attorney Rose Marie Doyle's plush office. When Aunt Goldie had died, she'd designated in her will that Ron take over as CEO of Silent Thunder. Doyle had documents to file and other details to handle before Ron could take an active role.

He was both excited and anxious to take over. Although, he still wasn't entirely certain of what he would be doing, he did know that the purpose of the trust was to help the poor or distressed. Goldie had been anonymously giving generous gifts to strangers for years. A reporter had picked up on the pattern of gift-giving and tried to figure out who the benefactor was, but to date had been unsuccessful. The reporter referred to his Aunt Goldie as the *Incognito Angel* because she had signed instruction letters with the initials IA. Goldie meant them to stand for Invisible Assistant, but when the reporter gave her the Angel name, she'd liked it better and used it herself.

Ron's timing was perfect. He reached Rose Marie's office with fifteen minutes to spare. He sat down in the waiting room and picked up a magazine to thumb through while he waited. The receptionist finally took him back to see Rose Marie. She had a Brooks Brothers fashion style, and her demeanor was as professional as her clothes. She didn't waste any time getting down to business.

"The paperwork is almost done, and Silent Thunder Charity will officially be yours and Sabre's," Rose Marie said. "In two weeks, you'll need to start taking an active role in the day-to-day running of the charity." She pointed at him when she said 'you.'

"What does that actually mean?"

"You will need to start looking for recipients for the gifts." She held up two fingers. "You're expected to do at least two a year, along with the RAKs."

"What are those?"

"Random acts of kindness. At first, Goldie insisted that they be done daily, but she loosened up after a while and required seven per week, making the accountability easier. You won't have to carry that burden yourself. The staff will help you." She made gestures as she talked, using her hands as much as her words.

"Counting you and Sabre, there are six of us. So, if you do two a week, we will each do one and the quota will be filled. Goldie used to do three or four and we covered the rest, but this splits it more evenly. But don't worry, your secretary will help you with that. And there's a program set up to record the RAK, so you can easily keep track of it on your phone."

"What are the parameters for the gifts?" Ron asked. "Amounts and such?"

"I'll give you a copy of the instructions. They're wide open, mostly limited by our budget. The principal of the foundation is to remain intact, with one exception." Again, with the finger. Ron remembered a schoolteacher who'd always done that. "If there's a loss for the charity, then salaries and gifts can come out of the principal. The gifts are centered around the return earned on the principal. Your budget is based on last year's earnings, which were pretty good. This year the market is down, so the return is lower. But Goldie left another five million to the charity, so we have a higher base to work from this year."

"You said there were six staff members. Who are they?"

"There's actually only five on staff. Raleigh, the stockbroker, is paid like he would be with any other account he handles. He doesn't actually know about the larger gifts, but he does do the RAKs. The staff consists of me, Corina Christiansen, the accountant/bookkeeper, Sandy Barnes, your secretary, and you and Sabre. We are paid a percentage of the earnings. Fifty percent goes to the big gifts, Corina gets two percent, Sandy gets five percent, and I get eight. Goldie used to take twenty-five percent, which will now be divided between you and Sabre. She gets five and you get twenty as acting CEO. All of these people make up the board, except Raleigh. And the board, of course, is privy to what the charity is all about. We have all signed non-disclosure statements, so no one will expose the charity."

"If my math is right, that still leaves ten percent."

"That ten percent goes for miscellaneous stuff like investigations, RAKs, and other minor gifts, supplies, that sort of thing."

"My main job is to find the people who will receive the gifts?"

"Your main purpose is to find those who need a boost in life and provide it for them. That could range from a free lunch at a drive through to a college education or a badly needed form of transportation."

Ron smiled. "I can do that."

"I know you can or Goldie wouldn't have picked you. You'll also have to investigate some, or hire it out, and file reports with the board for the big gifts."

Rose Marie brought up a list of the rules on her computer and printed it. She handed him the list. "There's a lot there, but the most important is to not support someone's drug or alcohol addictions. She has instituted a drug and alcohol testing protocol for the recipients. She wasn't concerned about social drinking, but she did not want to enable an alcoholic. Nor can anyone with a violent criminal record be a recipient. She was big on education, so there were lots of college tuitions or trade school gifts paid out. Over the years, she gave away cars, paid for weddings and honeymoons, and made down payments on starter homes. The important thing is to find someone in need who also has a good heart."

Ron felt his skin tingle as he thought about Aunt Goldie. His eyes blinked rapidly, followed by an open stare.

"What is it?" Rose Marie asked.

"Aunt Goldie was quite a woman. I wish I had known her better."

Chapter 14

Chapter 14

Wednesday early evening

Ron left the attorney's office and called JP to let him know he was working on the case. It was time to switch gears and put on his investigator's hat. He drove to the nearest Marshalls, located in Mission Valley. He spoke to several employees, including the manager, but found no trace of anyone named Melodi. From there he drove to the store on University. He found a girl named Melodi, but she was far too young to be the right person, and her name tag read MELODY, no 'I'. His next stop was the Marshalls on Midway in Point Loma, which put him closer to the strip clubs and his search for Belle.

The first employee Ron encountered was wearing a name tag. He decided to act as if he knew her and said, "Hi, Candace. Is Melodi here?"

He was surprised when she answered, "Yeah. She's in households."

"Thanks."

Ron was already walking away when she asked, "Do I know you?"

"No." Ron turned to face her. "I read your name tag."

She smiled and he headed to the correct department. He spotted a woman who looked to be about thirty, the right age. It took a few minutes to get into a position where he could see her name tag. Melodi, with an 'i'. *Bingo.* He wasn't sure what to do and didn't want to spook her, so he called JP for direction.

"What's up?" JP asked.

"I found a woman named Melodi who works at Marshalls. I don't know if it's the right one, but her name is spelled correctly."

"You haven't talked to her?"

"No. I wasn't sure you wanted me to."

"But she's still there?"

"At the moment. I suppose she could leave anytime."

"What store?"

"I'm in Point Loma."

"That's too far away for me to get to, and I'm in the middle of something. Don't talk to her yet. Hang outside and text me if she leaves."

Ron did as JP instructed and went to his car. He moved it twice before he had a good vantage point of the front door so he could see if she left. He didn't have to wait long. She walked out about twenty-five minutes later. He texted JP to let him know, all the while keeping an eye on Melodi.

Ron: *She's leaving.*

JP: *Follow her. Maybe she'll lead you to her house.*

Ron sent a thumbs up emoji.

The woman got into a gray Nissan and left the parking lot. Ron followed. She drove onto the I-8 freeway, heading east. She was easy to follow because she stayed in the right lane all the way to Spring Street. Ron followed her into an older neighborhood in La Mesa. She parked on the street in front of an apartment complex. Ron drove past and parked a few car lengths away. Several people strolled by. He got out and watched her walk to the backside of the apartments. He followed, but stepped into the stairwell so she couldn't see him. He peeked around the corner just in time to see what apartment she went into. Then texted JP.

Ron: *She went into an apartment on Lemon Street.*

JP: *Good work.*

Ron: *Do you want me to hang around and see if she goes anywhere else?*

JP: *No. Just send me the address and go see if you can find Belle.*

Before he returned to his car, Ron walked around to the other side of the building until he came to the mailboxes attached to the wall. He looked for the number of Melodi's apartment. The name on the box read, AKROYD. He sent JP the address, apartment number, and the name on the mailbox.

After he drove away, he stopped to get a burrito at a small Mexican restaurant nearby. He didn't want to start drinking on an empty stomach. Then he drove west on I-8, back in the direction he'd just come from. So much for good planning.

Ron called his friend Lana in Helena, Montana. They had a mutual friend, Tuper, who had introduced them. Lana was different from anyone he'd ever met, and he was crazy about her. Lana was a fiery redhead who wore combat boots and hacked into the web with great skill. She was feisty, independent, and a lot of fun. They had gotten close when he'd gone to Montana to spread Goldie's ashes, per her request. Unfortunately, it was difficult building a relationship at a distance. He hadn't seen her in over a month and wouldn't likely see her for a few more months at least. But he called her every few days when he wanted to share something with her. This was one of those times.

"Hey," she said, her standard greeting.

"Are you busy?"

"No. What's up?"

Ron wanted to tell Lana all about his trip to the attorney's office, but he couldn't, because it was a secret he needed to keep. Instead, he explained that he had been named in a paternity suit but that he couldn't be the father.

"That was unexpected information." Lana hesitated for a moment. "Is there anything I can do to help?"

"No. But thanks. As soon as the paternity test comes back, I'll be cleared."

Chapter 15

Chapter 15

Wednesday evening

JP entered the coffee shop, but didn't spot anyone he thought might be Katherine Jackson. He had told her to look for the guy with the black Stetson hat. He couldn't do that in Texas, but here, he was pretty sure he'd be the only one. A moment later, a striking blonde woman wearing knee-high boots walked in the door. She smiled when she saw him.

"You must be Katherine."

"JP?"

"Yes. Can I get you a coffee?"

"Please."

They stepped up to the counter. "Can I help you?" the clerk asked.

Katherine ordered first. "I'll have an iced venti café mocha macchiato with half and half and extra whipped cream."

"A medium black coffee for me."

JP paid, and a few minutes later, they took their drinks outside to sit.

"Thanks for meeting with me," JP said.

"Thelma was very persuasive."

"She sure spoke highly of you. She got quite attached to both you and Opal."

"As we did with her. What do you want to know?"

"Anything you can tell me about Ritchie Stadler."

"If it's about his dishonest business dealings, I don't know much except that he was a crook. If you want to know about him personally, that's a different story."

JP nodded. "Personal stuff it is."

"That I can do."

"You were with him for about a year, correct?"

"We dated for a couple of months before I moved in with him, and we lived together for eleven months. The worst mistake of my life."

"How so?"

"Ritchie is a horrible man, but you already know that, don't you?"

"I have my suspicions," JP said. "What was he like to live with?"

"He was generous and easy to get along with. I was struggling financially when we met. I was working full time and attending nursing school. I reached a point where I was going to have to quit for a while and save the money to go back, but he offered to pay for it. It wasn't even a loan. He just paid the tuition, straight out. I had a hard time accepting it at first, but he was very convincing."

"That was nice of him."

"I don't think so. Looking back, I think it was to get me out of the house more, so he had access to my daughter." She paused. "I'll tell you what I know, which really isn't a whole lot, but I will not do anything that involves my daughter or puts her in a situation where she has to tell anyone what happened to her. She's never even told me, but she was in therapy for a long time and seemed to open up with her counselor. We had some rough years. And although she is doing very well right now, she's at an age where she's really vulnerable. Do you understand?"

"Yes, ma'am. I respect that."

Katherine sipped her coffee, seeming to brace herself. "Ritchie was particularly attentive to Opal right from the start. He played with her, drove her to school, bought her ice cream cones, all normal things a father figure would do. I was so happy they seemed to be bonding, I didn't realize there may have been more." She shuddered. "I was so stupid."

"No. You weren't. He's the bad guy here. Not you."

She nodded. "One day I came home early and walked into the living room. They were sitting on the sofa watching TV, and when he saw me, he jerked his hand away from her lap. It took me a few seconds to understand what had happened. I didn't want to believe it at first, then I saw the look of pain on Opal's face and I knew."

"What did you do?"

"I didn't say anything. I simply took Opal by the hand and led her to her room. When we got there, I asked if she was uncomfortable around Ritchie. She said she didn't like the way he touched her. I wanted to go downstairs and bash his head in, but all I could think about was getting Opal as far away from him as I could. I took her suitcase out of the closet and told her to pack. I did the same, and we walked past him without saying a word."

"He didn't try to stop you?"

"Not until I reached the door. Then he jumped up and started to come toward us. He said, 'Let me explain. You misunderstood.' That sent me over the top. I dropped my suitcase and grabbed the gold and silver dragon statue that sat on a table near the entrance. I raised it and told him not to come any closer or I would bash his head in. Only I wasn't that polite about it. I used language I've never used in front of my daughter. He must've taken me seriously because he backed off. I dropped the statue, and we left."

"Did you ever see him or hear from him after that?"

"No. I went there the next day when he was at work. My brother and a friend helped me, and we picked up everything that belonged to me. I also took everything from Opal's room, the bed, the dresser, the pictures off the wall, everything. I completely stripped her room, even though he had bought most of the furniture." She paused to calm herself.

JP silently touched her hand and waited her out.

Finally, she continued. "I didn't want anything of Opal's left behind, and I didn't want the room furnished for another little girl he might bring home. I realize that wouldn't stop him from bringing another victim into his house, but at the time, it seemed like it would help. I wanted to destroy everything in that beautifully decorated home, including his model train room, but I didn't. Instead, I searched the house for any of my personal belongings, and on my way out I took that dragon."

"Was it yours?"

"Nope."

"Was it valuable?"

"Probably. He claimed it was, but that's not why I took it."

"Why did you?"

"Mostly because he loved it so much." She gave a devilish smile. "And I thought if he ever found us and dared to come around, I'd kill him with it."

Chapter 16

Wednesday night

Ron walked into The Legend on Rosecrans, a good starting point in his search. He hadn't been to a strip club in a decade or so. It had never really been his scene, but he'd gone a few times with friends. He ordered a beer and walked around, looking for a female employee who was a little older, maybe forty. Most of the strippers and waitresses were younger. He spotted a server who had a few years on the others and took a seat in her section. She was attractive, if you could get past the makeup. Her tight, skimpy uniform exposed her large breasts and accentuated her pudgy tummy and buttocks. In regular street clothes, she probably looked good, but the uniform wasn't flattering.

"What can I get for you, sugar?" she asked.

He ordered another beer, even though he hadn't drunk but a sip of the first one. He hadn't really thought that through. For some reason, he expected to get more information by ordering alcohol rather than a soft drink, which was probably silly. He made a mental note to ask JP what he thought. In the meantime, he would waste the beer.

When the waitress returned with his drink, Ron asked, "Have you worked here long?"

She sighed. "More of my life than I haven't."

Ron smiled at her answer. "Do you know if a woman named Belle ever worked here?"

"That's digging back a ways." She sighed again "Belle and I started around the same time and became close friends. We were both strippers then. I switched to waitressing about five years ago when my body started to get soft. Even though the money isn't as good, I prefer this work. I still get men pawing at me, but their expectations aren't as high for what else they want me to do."

"Is Belle still working here?"

"Oh no. She moved on years ago." The waitress took a seat at his table, which surprised him, but he didn't object. "She quit a few months after she started dating some rich guy in La Jolla. She thought it was her ticket out, but that didn't last long. She was back here within six months or so. She left again with some other jerk who started beating her and nearly ruined her pretty face. She came back to the club again after she healed. She was a customer favorite, so they always took her back. She seemed to attract men with money, but they were always a mess. Maybe that's why they were here looking for ... whatever they were looking for."

"How long did she stay that time?"

"Not long. She found another man to take care of her, and Belle didn't come back after that. At first, I thought she'd found her escape, but then I heard she had moved to another club."

"Do you remember which one?"

"She was at Déjà Vu for a while, but that didn't last long." She stood. "I'd better get back to work." She paused for a moment at the table. "Why are you looking for Belle?"

"Trying to help a friend," Ron said. "Thanks for the information."

"If you do find her, please tell her Jingles said hello."

"You bet. Thanks, Jingles."

Ron's next stop was Déjà Vu. It didn't take long to establish that Belle no longer worked there. The manager was helpful and took the time to check employee records. Belle had only worked there a year, then left. He had no information beyond that.

Ron hit two more bars with no success. It was nearly ten, and he was about done. He decided to check one more strip club because it was close by, then he'd call it quits for the night.

He walked into a place called *Bliss* and took a seat at the bar counter. Two women were on stage, working the poles. He wasn't totally comfortable in these bars, and although he didn't judge the women for their work, he still felt a little sorry for them. He figured for most; this wasn't their first choice.

He glanced around. Some of the women had really nice bodies, but most wore too much makeup for his taste. Personally, he preferred a more natural look. His mind drifted to Lana. He was totally attracted to her, and although she didn't wear much makeup, she wasn't what he would call a natural either. She had spiked dyed-red hair, a few piercings, and most likely at least one tattoo somewhere on her body. She wasn't his idea of the ideal woman, but there was something about her. Spunky, witty, and so much fun.

A woman walked up to him at the bar and interrupted his daydream. "Hey, daddy, want to buy me a drink before the show?"

Daddy? If he didn't know better, he would've guessed Bob had put her up to it. She looked quite young, so maybe he just looked old to her.

"Okay," he said, "but I'm only looking for information."

"Sure, honey." She ordered a drink, and Ron paid for it.

"What's your name?"

"Poodle."

"Nice to meet you, Poodle. I'm Ron. How long have you worked here?"

"About six months."

"Do you like the work?"

"It's not bad. It beats some of my other options."

Ron was trying to make her comfortable, but he seemed to be failing. Before he could ask her anything else, she said, "Please don't make the next question: What is a nice girl like you doing in a place like this?"

Ron smiled. "I wasn't going there. I have no problem with your choice of professions as long as you enjoy what you're doing."

"I don't, but it's getting me through beauty school."

"Good for you." He took a drink of his beer. "Do you know a woman named Belle?"

"Are you a cop or something?"

"I assure you; I am not."

"A killer?"

Ron laughed. "Not hardly."

"If you're looking for sex, she doesn't do that."

"So, you do know her."

Poodle studied him, but didn't say anything.

"I'm not looking for sex. I just need some information."

"From Belle?"

"Yes. She may be able to help a little girl who is in trouble."

"Thanks for the drink." The stripper stood. "She'll be here tomorrow. Her shift starts at seven."

Chapter 17

Thursday night

JP and Ron walked into the Bliss club together just before seven, hoping to catch Belle before she started her shift. They sat at the bar, and Ron looked around for Poodle. When he caught her eye, she approached them.

"Well, hello again."

"Hi, Poodle."

She looked JP up and down. "Who's the cowboy?"

Ron introduced them.

"So, which one of you boys is buying my drink?"

"I am," Ron said, a little too eagerly.

JP raised an eyebrow at him.

"Just protecting my sister's interest."

"Sure," JP said.

Poodle gestured to the bartender, and he brought her drink.

"Is Belle here?" Ron asked.

"I'll see if she'll talk to you. She doesn't go on for another fifteen minutes."

Poodle returned with a beautiful woman who looked about twenty-five.

"I should've asked her age," Ron whispered to JP.

"Yep. That definitely isn't our Belle."

Poodle introduced Belle, who immediately asked, "You looking for me?"

"We thought we were," JP said. "But you're too young to be the woman we need to talk to."

"You want someone older? That surprises me." She looked JP up and down. "Because, honey, you could have any woman you wanted."

JP was glad it was dark in the bar because he could feel his face flush. He didn't take compliments well, especially about his looks. "Thanks, but I just need to get some information."

"Maybe I can help." Belle smiled seductively at him.

"I don't think so. I'm really not lookin' for anything else. I'm trying to help young girls who are living in a bad environment. I think the older Belle might be able to shed some light on what happened years ago."

The young woman dropped her sensual demeanor. "I know. I mean, maybe I can give you the information you're looking for."

"Do you know the other Belle?"

"She was my mother."

"Was?" JP said sympathetically.

"She's been gone for years. And in spite of her efforts to get me to do otherwise, I followed in her footsteps." She shrugged. "Who am I kidding? The truth is she was a terrible mother. She worked hard, but she thought her job was to find a rich man to take care of us."

"And she couldn't do that?"

"The rich men who would take care of us were not nice guys. I don't know why she kept expecting them to be. We were poor white trash. What they wanted from us was never just love. She couldn't seem to get that through her head." A catch in her voice. "My mother was beautiful and that attracted them, but they either wanted to knock her around or abuse me." She looked JP directly in the eyes. "I hope that doesn't shock you, Cowboy."

"No. In fact, it makes me want to cancel a few birth certificates."

She and Poodle both laughed. Then Poodle said, "Thanks for the drink. I've got to get back to work." She hurried off.

"What did you want to know from my mother?" Belle asked.

"This goes back to when you were about five. Do you remember a man named Ritchie Stadler?"

"Oh yeah, the model train freak. I'll never forget that creepy room." She looked pensive. "He was the first. At least the first I can remember. He lived in a big house in La Jolla. I don't remember too much, but I know there was a playground next door and a nice old lady who lived there. I remember when we first moved into Ritchie's house, I thought I was in a castle, and I pretended to be a princess. We had been living on the streets before that, so it was quite a change. But it didn't take long before I wished we were back on the streets."

"Did Ritchie abuse your mother?"

"No. He was more interested in me. He was a real sicko, if you know what I mean."

"Do you remember why you left?"

"Oh yeah. I kept telling my mother what he was doing to me, but she kept making excuses for him. Finally, she left when he was showing more interest in me than her." Belle's tone softened. "I guess I shouldn't be so hard on her. She lived her life the only way she knew how. She just shouldn't have had a child."

"Thank you, Belle. You've been a big help."

She started to leave, then turned back. "You know, Cowboy, most people don't think much of me because of work. I could get a job in a restaurant serving food, or driving an Uber, or any respectable kind of work. But I couldn't make the kind of money I do here. I may have followed in my mother's footsteps, but I refuse to let any man take care of me. I live my life the way I choose without depending on anyone else. I won't bring a child into this world for lots of reasons, but mostly because I'd make a lousy mother, and I know that. I also know this job will only pay well while I maintain my figure and keep my looks. So, I save every dollar I can and someday, at the ripe old age of forty or so, I'll retire. Most people can't do that."

"I believe you will, darlin'. Good for you."

"Over the years, I've cleaned up more of my mother's messes than I want to talk about. There's only one left to take care of."

"What's that?"

"It doesn't matter." She smiled. "I have an ace in the hole. My mother left me something very valuable."

"Really? What?"

"Knowledge. I won't make the same mistakes she did."

Chapter 18

Friday morning

JP knocked on the door of the apartment where Ron had seen Melodi. JP recognized the woman who answered the door from the photographs Ron had taken when he spotted her at Marshalls. It was definitely the same woman.

"Hi, ma'am. My name is JP Torn. I'm a private investigator. I'd like to ask you a couple of questions."

"Go away." She reached for the door to close it.

"Please, ma'am. It's very important. You may be able to help a child in danger." He never quite knew what to say to get through, but saving children did the trick more often than not.

Melodi stepped outside and closed the door behind her. "What do you want?" She spoke harshly.

"I just want to ask a couple of questions about Ritchie Stadler."

"I knew it!" She threw her arms up in the air. "I can't do this. My daughter can't do this. And my husband sure as hell isn't going to take any more of this. Just leave us alone."

"Has someone already questioned you?"

"A social worker was here this morning, and my husband is furious. He knew nothing about what happened until now, and he's not taking it well. Please just leave before he wakes up."

"I understand." JP handed her a card. "Please call if I can help in any way."

She stuck the card in her pocket, stepped inside, and closed the door without responding. JP was certain the card would hit the nearest trashcan.

That went well.

~~~

JP returned to his home office and commenced a search for Izzy Hernandez. Izzy was likely a nickname, so he ran everything under Izzy, Elisabeth, and Isabelle, with various spellings. There were more names that might have prompted that nickname, but those were the most likely. Her surname wasn't much help because it was so common, and he had to run it with two spellings, one with a 'z' and one with an 's.' He started with social media, but there were just too many hits. And for all he knew, the woman in question had a different last name by now. He gave up and ran her name through a criminal check.

He narrowed the criminal search down to three Elizabeths and two Isabelles who were the right age and had been convicted in California. No Izzys. He was able to eliminate one Isabelle who had spent her whole life in Northern California. The charges for the other four ranged from drug possession and prostitution to armed robbery and manslaughter. He dropped their rap sheets into a folder on his computer and started in another direction.

Obituaries often narrowed his search. So, that's where he went next. The first and most recent obit was for an Elizabeth Hernandez, but she had died at seventy-four. The next was a teenager who'd died from a drug overdose. The third was a one-liner. *Elizabeth "Izzy" Hernandez, age thirty-seven, murdered.* He checked the date, only two months earlier. He started a google search.

Two hours later, JP spotted what he was looking for. The article read:
~~~

The death of a woman found on the beach is being investigated as a homicide, police said. The body was discovered early Sunday morning on the sand in Imperial Beach, police said in a statement. The woman appeared to be in her thirties or forties. Homicide detectives were called because there was no explanation for her death and because of the unusual circumstances surrounding her location.

JP continued to search and found a follow-up story.

Body of woman found on the sand in Imperial Beach was determined to be Elizabeth Hernandez. She was identified by her daughter, Natalie Hernandez. Elizabeth had an extensive history of prostitution and drug convictions. The homicide unit is investigating, but have not revealed any likely leads.

He found nothing after that about the woman or her murder. Her death apparently wasn't newsworthy since she was likely considered *just another prostitute.*

JP closed his folder on Izzy and wondered what Natalie's life had been like. She probably hadn't gotten many breaks along the way. It didn't seem fair, but JP had learned at a very young age that life wasn't fair.

Chapter 19

Chapter 19

Friday morning

Ron drove Sabre to court so he could borrow her car for the morning. They pulled into the parking space next to Bob, who was just getting out of his car.

"You have an Uber driver this morning?" Bob asked.

"Yup. We dropped off Ron's car at the mechanic. We'll pick it up after court this morning."

"Hi, Bob," Ron said.

"Hi, baby daddy."

"Funny guy. But I'll get the last laugh. I know I'm good, but to reach a thousand miles is a stretch even for me."

Bob became serious. "Do you know Carla's sister, Emma?"

"It's been a while, but I saw quite a bit of her when Carla and I were dating. She and her husband, Roger, were both nice people. I remember they wanted to have children, but she couldn't get pregnant. Did they ever have any?"

"No. But according to the social worker, they've practically raised your kid."

"She's not mine."

"Oh, that's right. I forgot." Bob grinned.

"You're going to keep this up until the test comes back, aren't you?"

"You bet, daddy."

Sabre cut in. "What do you mean Emma raised Liberty?"

"Apparently, Carla had a breakdown after Liberty was born, so Emma and Roger kept the baby while she was away. After she was released, Carla lived with them for almost three years." A car flew past them in the parking lot, and Bob gestured at them without missing a beat. "Liberty called Emma 'mama' before she called Carla that. Carla got better and was doing so well she moved out, but she got a place only a few blocks from her sister. Emma and Roger finally felt like they could take a vacation. Now, they're sorry they did."

"Are they back home?" Sabre asked.

"Yes. They were able to get on a redeye and returned yesterday morning. Their home was evaluated, and Liberty was detained with them by afternoon."

"Is Carla okay with that?"

"Yes, she's fine with it. She says they've been better parents than she could be. She doesn't seem to have any animosity about that."

"It's good that Liberty is in a familiar place with people who love her," Sabre added.

Bob looked at Ron. "Of course, if the baby daddy would step up and do the responsible thing..."

Ron rolled his eyes. "This is all fun and games, but I have to go. Call me when you're done, Sabre, if I'm not back already."

Bob and Sabre walked into the courthouse and went their separate ways. Sabre checked her mailbox, but there were no new reports. In Department One, she perused her morning calendar. She had four cases, all reviews, and none that should take long. She was right. Thirty minutes later, she headed to Department Five for a delinquency case, then hurried to Department Four. Bob was waiting when she got there.

"Is this your last case?" he asked.

"Yes. How about you?"

"This is it for me too. If Ron's not back when we're done, I can take you to your office."

"He shouldn't be long. I'll text him when we finish," Sabre said. "What are you doing on this case?"

"A trial set."

"Good. That'll be quick."

Sabre represented the child this time, a twelve-year-old boy who wanted to live with his father, Bob's client. The mother had extensive drug history. The father, on the other hand, seemed to be a sex-addict. The mother had accused him of having a great deal of porn and questionable sexual partners. In the dad's defense, none of the porn had anything to do with minors, and the sex partners were all consenting adults. In every other aspect, he appeared to be a great father. He spent as much time as he could with his son. He was manager of a local sporting goods store and paid child support on time. He took his son into his home whenever the mother was on a binge or in jail.

Sabre welcomed the trial, hoping they could get enough information to determine where the child should live. The judge set the trial for three weeks ahead.

"I'm going to check my mailbox," Bob said. "I'll meet you out front."

"Grab mine too, please."

Bob raised his hand in acknowledgment as he walked away.

Sabre approached the social worker to discuss a few things on the case. Just as she finished her conversation, she received a text from Ron saying he had arrived.

Sabre gathered up her files and went in the direction of the attorney lounge. Bob met her halfway and handed her a couple of documents from her mailbox, then went back to reading his own report.

"Thanks."

Ron met them at the front door. "You ready?" he asked, as he reached for her files.

"Yup."

"Wait." Bob stopped walking and handed Sabre the report.

"What's this?"

Bob had a serious look on his face. "It's the paternity results on Carla's case."

Sabre smiled and shook her head "You're still trying to make us think Ron's the father. The joke's getting old."

"No joke," Bob said. "Read it."

Sabre glanced at the numbers. *Ninety-nine percent probability.* Eyes wide, she looked up at Ron.

He grabbed the paper. "How is it possible?"

"Let me tell you about the birds and the bees," Bob said, back to his humorous self.

"I mean it," Ron protested. "I haven't had sex with Carla in eight years. The kid is only four. It doesn't make sense."

"Are you sure you didn't run into her and have a quick roll in the hay?" Bob asked.

"I was out of state, remember? There is no way this is possible."

"Maybe you were drunk and don't remember?" Bob teased.

"I haven't been that drunk since I was in college. I would know if I slept with the woman. That's not something you just forget. Maybe if it was a one-night stand, but I had a relationship with her for years. I'm telling you I did not sleep with her five years ago. I wasn't even around." He turned to Sabre. "You believe me, don't you?"

Sabre paused for a split second.

"You don't believe me?" Ron looked hurt.

"Of course, I do. I'm just trying to wrap my head around how this could've happened."

Chapter 20

Sabre sat at the breakfast table with her family, drinking a cup of tea. The rest were eating breakfast, with Conner gulping down his food.

"Slow down, kid," JP said. "You're moving faster than a prairie fire with a tail wind."

"Sorry. I don't want to be late."

"We won't be," JP assured him.

Conner finished his last bite, drank his orange juice, and stood. "Excuse me."

JP nodded. "That kid eats entirely too fast."

"He was worse than normal," Sabre added.

"I'm done too." Morgan got up. "I'm ready when you are, Uncle Johnny."

"I know, Sweetie. You were ready before the rooster crowed this morning."

"We don't have a rooster." The girl smiled. "You're funny."

"If we did have a rooster, you would've been the one to wake him up this morning."

"I'll wait in the living room."

Sabre smiled. "I'm not sure which of those two is the most excited about seeing their dad."

"It's been a while."

"I know, and Morgan is worried the prison might be on shutdown again like the last time."

"I sure hope not," JP said. "Both of them will be hugely disappointed." JP pondered. "You know, my brother may not have done much right in his life, but he sure loved his kids."

"And he made sure they knew it," Sabre said. "They respect him too."

"I just hope Conner doesn't respect him too much. I'd hate to see him go down the same path."

"He won't. He's a good kid, and he respects you too. You're a great example for him."

"I hope so." JP stood. "What's on your agenda today?"

"Dené and I are getting pedicures. We had planned to grocery shop for Thanksgiving, but since my mom and Harley offered to make dinner, I gladly acquiesced."

"Who all is going for Thanksgiving?"

"There will be the five of us, Ron, Harley and Mom, and she invited Travis."

"None of Harley's kids will be there?"

"No, the two oldest are spending the holiday with their families, and Chloe, his youngest, is skiing in Aspen."

"And it's not too much for your mom?"

"No. She's thrilled. She loves entertaining in that big, beautiful home, and Harley is great about helping." Sabre was lost in thought for a second. "Mom sure seems happy since she met Harley."

"She does. I'm happy for her." JP changed the subject. "I hate to take the time to do this today. Don't get me wrong, you know I love seeing Gene, but I have so much to do on your cases, and now this paternity thing with Ron."

Sabre looked off into space.

"Sabre?"

"I'm sorry. It'll all be there tomorrow."

"What's bothering you?"

"I can't wrap my head around the fact that Ron has a child. That means I have a niece. One I may never get to know.

I can't let Ron know how I feel because I don't want to influence his decision. He has to do what's best for him."

They heard the kids' anxious chatter in the living room.

JP peeked around the corner. "I'd better get going before Morgan wears a hole in the rug. She can't seem to sit still, and she's talking an ear off Conner."

Sabre kissed him. "Have fun."

When they left, Sabre poured another cup of tea and sat down in the living room to relax. Dené was sleeping in. Sabre sat back and enjoyed the silence. She thought about turning on some music, but decided the quiet was what she needed right now.

Her peaceful moment was interrupted when her cell rang. She glanced at the screen and saw it was the social worker on the Harn/Stadler case. *The social worker calling on a Saturday. This couldn't be good.* She hoped her client hadn't done anything stupid.

"Hello," Sabre said.

"This is Nikki Roe, the social worker on the Harn/Stadler case. I'm sorry to bother you on the weekend, but I thought you should know what happened."

"What?" Sabre asked nervously.

"Ritchie Stadler is dead. He's been murdered."

"Oh no. How? Who?"

"We don't know much yet. A co-worker found him this morning in his bed. His associate was there to pick Stadler up for a meeting in Los Angeles."

"They're sure it was murder?"

"He took a fatal blow to the head which caused a brain bleed. The word *devil* was written in marker across the mirror. Yeah, I'd say he was murdered."

Chapter 21

Chapter 21

Saturday night

Sabre and Dené were sitting in a small Mexican restaurant having an early dinner when JP called. "The kids and I are stopping at In-N-Out. Should we bring something for you and Dené?"

Sabre checked the time. The cops were questioning Grady at 7:30, and she had agreed to be there. She wanted to talk to her client beforehand, so she was scheduled to meet him at 6:30. JP had plenty of time to get home, then go back out with her. "No thanks. We're eating now and almost done."

"Good," JP said. "Then no one has to make dinner tonight. How did your day go?"

"It was fine. I'll tell you about it when you get home. By the way, we have something we need to do at 6:30, if you can."

"What?"

"I'll tell you *that* when you get home too." Sabre didn't want to get into it over the phone, and the less the kids heard about their cases the better off they were.

She and Dené finished their meal and drove home, arriving about five minutes before JP and the other kids returned.

"How did it go?" Sabre asked.

Conner smiled. "It was nice to see Dad." He walked off to his room.

"It was stupendous," Morgan said.

"Her word for the day," JP said.

"I figured."

Morgan ignored them and went on jabbering in her usual fashion. "Dad was so happy to see us. We got to sit outside in this yard where families meet with the inmates. Dad has been on good behavior, so he can do more now than the last time we saw him. I know he's looking forward to getting out of there, but he says all the right stuff. He claims it's not so bad, and that the food is better than what Mom used to make, except for the biscuits, which he called 'dobies'. I asked him why he called them that, and he said because they're like adobe bricks. He gets lots of exercise, and he doesn't mind his job. It makes the time pass quicker, he says. He's considered a short timer, so there's a lot of jobs he can't do, but he's okay with that. They give some of the nasty jobs to the fish, that's the guys who just came to prison and have no friends. They're not treated very nice. My dad's not a fish because even though he went back in not long ago, he was there before. So, he knows the ropes." Without a pause, Morgan asked, "How was your day? Did you and Dené get your pedicures? Maybe I can go next time, but seeing Dad was better."

"I'm sure it was," Sabre said. "Next time we'll plan it so you can go." She was happy that Morgan got to see her father but hated that the young girl was speaking prison lingo. Not that the words mattered. It was just that she was in a situation that forced her to learn them. She should've been talking about Disney movies and Barbie dolls, not prison visits.

"Thanks." Morgan gave Sabre a quick kiss on the cheek and ran off. She didn't do that kind of thing very often, so Sabre was a little surprised. "I'm not sure what that was about."

"I think she's just thankful to be here," JP said. "She talked about that on the way home." He took her hand. "Now, how was your day, really?"

"Spending the day with Dené was nice and we needed it."

"But?"

"Someone murdered Ritchie Stadler."

"Wow. I didn't see that coming," JP said. "Although, I probably should have. There are plenty of people who would like to see him dead. Is your client a suspect?"

"I'm sure he is or will be. That's who we're meeting with at 6:30. The homicide detective is coming to meet with him at 7:30. I thought we could question Grady first and decide whether he should talk to the police. He doesn't live far from here, but we have to go soon. Are you okay with that?"

"I was hoping to take off my boots and kick back, but this is good too."

"I'll check with Conner and see if he can stay with the girls."

"I'm sure he will. He said he wasn't going anywhere tonight."

"He's very good about watching them. I just don't want to take advantage of him. He's spent most of his life watching out for Morgan, and it would be nice if he could just be a teenager before he isn't anymore."

"If he's busy, I can stay home."

"Oh no you don't. I've already made arrangements with Ron to cover if Conner can't."

"I'll check with Conner." JP left and returned a moment later. "Let's go. I need to stop and fill the gas tank."

Once on the road, JP asked, "Do you think your client is capable of killing the creep?"

"I hope not. But he's pretty angry about what Stadler did to his daughter." She looked over at JP. "What would you do if you were in his shoes?"

"He would've been buzzard bait long before now."

Chapter 22

Chapter 22

Saturday night

Sabre, JP, and Grady sat in his modest living room. It was completely furnished, but lacked pictures or art on the walls. Overall, it was clean, but a newspaper lay on an end table next to a paper plate with some crumbs. Sabre talked to Grady about his daughter and the visit they'd had yesterday.

"The social worker mentioned lifting my supervision next week. Do you think this will affect her decision?"

"That depends on whether you're a suspect. If you are, the supervised visits will stay in place."

"Why? I'd never hurt my daughter."

"Even if they believe that, they'd be afraid you would run with her."

"That's crazy." Her client stood and started pacing. "The man is dead and he's still hurting my little girl."

"Please calm down," Sabre said. "You can't display that kind of emotion when the detective gets here."

"I...I know."

"I need to ask you some questions that the cops are sure to ask. Please be truthful with me. After we talk, we can decide how to proceed."

"Go ahead."

"Did you kill Stadler?" Sabre had to ask.

"No. I did not. I can't say I'm sorry he's dead, but I didn't do it. I'd like to know who it was so I could shake their hand, but I swear it wasn't me."

"It might be best if you don't say all that to the detectives when they question you."

"I know."

"The murder took place last night around eleven," Sabre said. "The first thing they will check is to see if you have an alibi."

"I don't."

"Where were you?"

"Right here watching *The Monk*."

"Alone?"

"Yes, ma'am."

"Have you had any contact with Stadler since that day in court?"

"No."

"Have you ever been inside his house?" Sabre continued.

"A couple of times when I picked up Dakota. Twice, I think."

"So, there's an explanation if they find your DNA in there."

"I guess."

"Did you go anywhere or do anything last night? Trace your steps from about five o'clock."

"I went right home after work. I did a few things in my garage, ate some dinner, and relaxed. It was an uneventful evening."

Sabre looked at JP. "Do you have any questions?"

"Have you ever threatened Stadler?" JP asked.

"Not verbally. At least I don't think I have. I've certainly thought it enough, so it's possible. And I attacked him in court, which I know was really stupid. But he smiled when the allegations were read, and I wanted to wipe that look off his ugly mug."

"Sabre mentioned that." JP tipped his head. "Not your best move. But think, have you ever told your daughter you would kill him or wanted to kill him?"

"No. I'm sure I didn't do that."

"What about your ex-wife?"

Grady thought for a moment. "That's possible. I couldn't understand how she could stick with him. But she's back on her own now, so maybe that'll bring her to her senses."

"What about neighbors or friends? Have you talked to anyone who might report comments you made?"

"Not really. I don't share much of my personal life. My family, of course, knows what's going on. I've vented to my brother mostly, but I doubt he'd ever repeat anything I said." Her client finally sat back down. "If I threatened to kill Stadler, and I probably did, Tyler would never tell because he knows I wouldn't really do it. I'm the sensitive one in the family. I'd never hurt an animal or go to war." Grady paused, then said, "In fact, I did say something to him, and he gave me a lecture. He said it leaves a big hole inside when you take a life."

JP's eyes narrowed. "Has your brother ever killed someone?"

"He's an ex-marine. He did a tour in Iraq, and it was pretty bad. He didn't talk about it much, but once in a while he'd make a comment like that, so I'm sure he did."

"Would you mind if we talked to your brother?"

"Not if you think it might help."

"We just want to stay ahead of the detectives in case they talk to him. You said his name is Tyler?"

"Yes." Grady gave his brother's information. JP had just finished writing it down when the doorbell rang.

"Do you want me to get that?" Sabre asked.

"Yes, please." Grady turned back to JP. "They're not going to arrest me, are they?"

"As far as we know, they have no physical evidence. So, it's unlikely, unless they have something we don't know about," JP said.

"They shouldn't have any evidence against me because I didn't do it."

"Then you're probably good."

"Before they come in, do you know of anyone who would want Stadler dead?"

"My guess would be anyone who ever met him."

Sabre opened the door. A young man in cowboy boots said, "I'm Detective Barry Wells."

"Please come in," Sabre said. She explained who she was, introduced JP, and indicated she and JP would stay for the questioning. She estimated Wells' height at about five-eleven after she removed a couple of inches for the boots. Wells was muscular, but his brown, wavy hair gave him a boyish look. And the small mole over his right eye seemed to jump when he smiled.

The detective asked similar questions to those they had rehearsed, and this time Grady didn't editorialize. He denied any culpability and offered to help in any way he could. Sabre was a little surprised at how well he maintained his composure. Maybe the practice was all he needed. Wells left without arresting him.

On the way home, Sabre asked, "Do you think Grady did it?"

"It's possible. It was interesting the way he answered the question about his ex-wife, saying this might 'bring her to her senses.' Let's hope he wasn't helping her get there."

"So, you think he did it?"

"No. But I haven't ruled him out. Stadler had a bucket load of people who wanted him dead, so there are a lot of likely suspects. I'll start looking first thing in the morning. My first stop will be with Dakota's Uncle Tyler."

Chapter 23

Chapter 23

Sunday morning

JP sat in the backyard, drinking a cup of coffee, and waiting for Ron. He'd called and asked if he could come over and discuss something. When Ron arrived, he joined JP on the deck with his own cup of coffee. They exchanged pleasantries and sat in silence for about thirty seconds.

"I need your help," Ron said.

"The Carla issue?"

"I need you to find out who the real father is."

"The test says it's you."

"But it isn't. I don't know how the result came up the way it did, but I swear it's not me."

"There's only so many ways they could get that outcome," JP said. "One, if someone rigged the test. But why would anyone do that? *Who* would do that? And how would they have access to it? Maybe the social worker had limited access, but I can't imagine she would do that because she has nothing to gain. Carla has the most to gain, but I can't see how she would have the means."

"She's more resourceful than you may think."

"What do you mean?"

"She always had a way of getting things done we thought were impossible."

"Like what?"

"We went to a fancy restaurant once that you had to book months in advance. We didn't have a reservation, but she talked her way in. Twice, she got stopped for traffic violations but didn't get a ticket either time. There are other examples that I can't think of right now, but she has a knack for figuring ways into places, or out of messes."

"Then we won't rule her out," JP said. "Who else would have anything to gain?"

"The real father."

"But we don't know who that is. The only person Carla has named is you."

"What about the aunt and uncle? They want to raise the child."

"Then they'd be better off if you weren't the father, correct?"

"I guess you're right." Ron was silent for a moment. "Unless they thought I'd sign away parental rights and that would be one less hurdle to jump over."

"That's way too risky. You're sounding like a bad soap opera."

"I guess I did get a little carried away. What is the second possibility?"

"If there was a mistake of some sort. It's highly unlikely, but it shouldn't be too hard to investigate and follow the chain. I'll do some research on what makes a false positive."

"And the third way?"

"It's actually a match."

"But that can't be," Ron protested. "I haven't had sex with her."

"Could she have gotten your sperm and used it?"

"You mean, came to Washington, found me, got my sperm without me noticing, and impregnated herself with it? Just so she could have my baby? That's nuts."

JP raised an eyebrow.

"That's crazy even for Carla. It doesn't make any sense."

JP wanted to make a joke, but decided Ron was too stressed to handle it. "I'll see what I can find out. I'll check the validity of the test to make sure there were no chain-of-evidence issues. I'll also do what I can to find out if everyone handling the sample was competent."

"Can you question Carla? Just to see where she's coming from?"

"No. But there's no reason *you* can't talk to her. Just don't intimidate her or anything."

"I'd never do that."

"And you'd better check with Sabre first to make sure she thinks it's okay."

"I will."

Sabre walked up. "Check with me about what?"

"Talking to Carla about the paternity. JP said it was okay, but not to intimidate her, which I would never do."

"We'll give Bob a heads up. He may want to be there with you. Technically, there is no reason you can't talk to her. There's no restraining order or anything, but she's fragile so let's go through Bob first. You don't need a new set of problems on your hands."

"Fair enough." Ron looked down at his feet, then back up again. "None of this makes any sense. You have to believe me, Sis. I'm not the father of Carla's baby. There has to be some mistake."

"I believe you, but it's hard to get around a paternity test that says ninety-nine point nine percent *likelihood*."

"It actually says *not excluded as the biological father.* Maybe there are other men who are *not excluded* as well."

"The only way that's possible is if you have an identical twin brother."

Ron's eyes widened.

"Which you don't," Sabre said with an edge in her voice. "There is no way our mother gave birth to twins and gave one up."

"Maybe he was stolen, and Mom doesn't know about him."

Sabre shook her head. "Do you realize how ludicrous you sound?"

"I'm just trying to understand how this could happen. I swear to you, I'm not the father of this child." Ron sighed. "Maybe I fall into the other one percent."

"It's actually ninety-nine point nine, nine, nine, nine percent, so you would have to fall into the other point zero, zero, zero, one percent," Sabre added "They run matches for fifteen or twenty DNA markers. If you're the father, all fifteen will match. Yours did."

"Then why don't they say one hundred percent? And why use the term *not excluded?"*

"To get 100%, they would have to test the entire genome of an individual—all of their DNA."

"So, let's do that."

"It's not feasible. First, it would cost tens of thousands of dollars. Second, we'd have to get a court order to test Liberty, which is never going to happen."

JP jumped in to ease the tension between the siblings. "I told Ron I would check on the testing process to make sure there was no mistake or tampering."

"Thank you," Sabre said. She leaned over and kissed Ron on the cheek. "I do believe you, Bro. We'll figure this out." She walked back in the house.

"I'll get on this as soon as I can," JP said. "But right now, I have to find out who killed Stadler."

"Do you have any suspects?"

"Unfortunately, we have too many, but no real evidence, just motives and hunches."

"Could it be one of the victims' mothers that we've been looking for and talking to?"

"It's certainly possible. But why now? After so long?"

"Maybe *we* triggered it by bringing up the past."

"I thought about that," JP mused. "But it doesn't seem likely. There are just so many."

"Put me in, coach. I'll help in any way I can."

"I just may do that, but right now I'm going to see a marine about a war."

~~~

Before JP went to see Grady's brother, he stopped to see Thelma, on the chance she had witnessed something the night of her neighbor's death.

"It's so nice to see you again. Please come in." She stepped back, smiling.

"Thanks. But I don't have long. I just want to ask some questions about Stadler. Did you hear what happened?"

"I saw all the emergency vehicles yesterday morning. I felt bad for that poor young man who found him dead like that. Then Heidi came home, and I heard her scream. Shortly after, the police started showing up. I didn't go over because I figured there wasn't anything I could do."

"Did you know Heidi would be gone Friday night?"

"Yes. She told me that afternoon she was going to her mother's for the night."

"Were you in their house on Friday?"

"No. She came over here."

"Did she do that often?" Camden came up to JP and rubbed against his leg, but took off again before he could be petted.

"He'll get used to you. Pretty soon he'll be on your lap." Thelma said. "To answer your question. Heidi never comes over without a reason, but maybe she was just lonely with her daughter gone."

"Maybe." JP wondered if Heidi had been establishing an alibi. "Did you see or hear anything unusual that night?"

"Like I told the cops, I'm up and down like a yo-yo all night long. I saw someone walking toward my house, but I don't know if he came out of the Stadler house."

"Any idea what time?"
~~~

"12:34."

"You know the exact time?"

"I always look at the clock when I wake up. Then I count the time I have left to sleep and decide if it's worth going back to bed."

The phone rang, and Thelma excused herself to answer it. When she returned, she said, "That was my daughter. She worries too much, but this time she has some reason to, I guess." Thelma touched the side of her face. "I'm sure you noticed my bruise. I was moving too fast and took a tumble the other day. Now my daughter doesn't want me out of her sight."

"Did you get hurt anywhere else?" JP asked with concern.

"Just a few more bruises on my arms and legs. That's what happens when you get old. You bruise if you get hit with a feather." She smiled. "Where were we?"

"You said 'he' was walking by. You knew it was a man?"

"I'm not sure. He or she was dressed all in black or dark colors, and I only got a glimpse before he disappeared past my house. They had a long object in their hand, but I have no idea what it was." She gestured to show the length, about a foot. "A few moments later, a white car drove past."

"What did it look like? Was it a sedan, or a van, or ...?"

"It was an SUV. That I remember."

"What direction did it come from?"

"The same direction as the person was walking. So, he could've gotten in his car and driven away, or it could've been someone different all together. I know that's not much help."

"Maybe more than you know," JP said.

Chapter 24

Chapter 24

Sunday early afternoon

JP drove to the address Grady had given him for his brother. The garage door was open, and a man stood near the work bench. When JP walked up, he stopped what he was doing and laid down the tool.

"Are you Tyler Harn?" JP asked.

"Yes."

"My name is JP Torn. I'm a private investigator."

The man reached out to shake JP's hand. "Grady told me you'd be coming. Nice to meet you."

"You too. I understand you're a fellow marine."

"Semper fi."

"Semper fi. You served in Iraq?"

"I did," Tyler said. "Were you there too?"

"Desert Storm. I was just a kid at the time. It's a hard thing to get over."

"I know that, Brother." Tyler's solemn look changed to a smile, and he asked, "How can I help Grady? That's why you're here, right?"

"Mostly. Grady said he told you about the juvenile court case, including that the perpetrator was murdered."

"He did. I feel so bad for Dakota. She's a sweet kid and already struggling with her parents being divorced. She didn't need anything else."

"Are you close to Dakota?"

"She's my only niece, the only girl in the family. I have two boys, so she's the family princess."

"I haven't had the pleasure of meeting her yet, but I've only heard good things. We'd hate to see her lose her dad too, so we're trying to find out what happened to Stadler. Grady may be a prime suspect in the case, although that hasn't been stated by the police yet. We're just trying to get ahead of it and make sure he isn't blamed for something he didn't do."

"So, you believe him when he says he didn't kill the guy?"

"Do you?"

"Without a doubt. There's no way my brother would've killed him. Granted, he's angrier than I've ever seen him, but he couldn't kill anyone. Grady is just not a violent guy." Tyler used a dismissive gesture. "I know he went after that pervert in court, but that was impulse, and he didn't really hurt him. The way this sounds, he would've had to plan it, seek him out, and bash his head in. That's just not Grady."

"Could you have done it?"

"I could have," Tyler said without hesitation, while he looked JP directly in the eyes. "I've killed before. Under the right circumstances, I'm sure I could do it again, but I didn't."

"Do you have an alibi?"

"Am I a suspect?"

"Not as far as I know. But the cops might start looking at you next."

"I was home with my wife and kids."

"Good to know." JP thanked him and walked off.

Tyler called after him, moving in his direction.

JP stopped and turned. "Yes?"

"I would never let Grady go down for something I did."

"I expect you wouldn't, brother."

JP wondered if that was Tyler's way of saying he'd done it but would come forward to save Grady. Or maybe he was just making sure JP knew how important they were to each other. Either way, Tyler was definitely still on his list.

~~~

JP went back to the Stadler neighborhood in La Jolla and questioned other neighbors but didn't learn much. No one had seen or heard anything. So, JP went home to regroup and set up a plan. Every one of Stadler's victims and their families had a motive for killing him. Although most of the crimes had happened long ago, which would beg the question: *Why now?* On top of that, Stadler had made enemies at work and probably everywhere he went. JP couldn't discount the people Stadler had cheated out of money, which would be considerably more difficult to investigate. Hopefully, the homicide detectives would get that done.

JP made a list of the women Thelma had told him about. Although Izzy and Belle were dead, their daughters, Natalie and Belle were possibilities. Then there was Katherine and her daughter Opal, and Melodi and her daughter Paige, who was probably too young. He crossed her off. Of course, there was Heidi, but she was unlikely since she was still with the guy. She apparently believed him. JP hated to think it might be Katherine. He really liked her. Then there were Grady and Tyler. JP didn't like any of the possible outcomes. These were all people whose lives had been negatively affected by the monster. He couldn't blame any of them. His thoughts were interrupted when Sabre walked in.

"Are you getting anywhere?" she asked.

"Not really. Everyone on my list has a good reason for offing the guy. I just need to start checking alibis and see if I can narrow the search. It's such a wide net. His co-workers didn't like him, although probably not enough to kill him. He has apparently bilked a lot of people out of money, and that always makes a good motive. Especially considering the large amounts he seemed to deal with regularly. Not to mention his molest victims, which adds another whole layer."
~~~

"Do you have any hunches?"

"No. And I don't have any evidence. I don't know the detective on the case, so it'll be difficult to get information."

"What about Vinny DuBois? He's still a homicide detective, isn't he?"

DuBois was an old friend and colleague who always referred to JP as McCloud. They went way back, and DuBois would help if he could. "That's a good idea. I'll give him a call. Maybe he can put in a word for me, at the very least."

"You know you don't have to prove who did it. You just need to prove it wasn't my client."

"I know, but it's hard to prove a negative. The best way to make sure he isn't charged and convicted is to prove it was someone else."

"Grady will likely become their number one suspect, and he swears he didn't do it."

"Yeah, and Ron claims he's not the father of that baby," JP said. "I'm sorry. There's just so much that's not adding up."

Sabre ignored the comment about Ron. "They have no real evidence against Grady."

"That we know of," JP said. "By the way, do you know what kind of car Grady drives?"

"An SUV. Mazda, I think."

"It wouldn't happen to be white, would it?"

"Yes, why?"

"Thelma saw a white SUV in her neighborhood around 12:30. It's probably nothing. Half the cars on the road these days are white SUVs."

"Right. So, all you have to do is find who really did it, assuming it wasn't him, then we can clear him, and he can get custody of his child. We know any of those women Stadler wronged could've done it. And who knows how many more there are that we don't know about? And then there's the dozens or hundreds of people whose money he scammed.

Piece of cake. I know you can do it, sweetheart." She kissed him lightly on the cheek.

"I think I'll start with Melodi again. She's reluctant to talk to me, but I think she's warming up."

"Didn't she close the door in your face last time?"

"Yeah, but she didn't slam it, so we've got that going for us."

Chapter 25

Sunday late afternoon

JP knocked on Melodi's door. No one answered. He was about to knock again when he saw her moving slowly up the stairs carrying two bags of groceries. He met her halfway down the steps.

"Let me help you with those."

She handed him one without really looking at him. Then he held out a hand to help her up the steps. "Thanks."

"Sure."

Her stomach protruded and she looked pregnant. *How did he not notice that before?* He thought about the last visit, when she was wearing a baggy sweatshirt. He didn't mention it in case he was wrong. "You look tired. Are you okay?"

"I'm fine. I don't know why they call it *morning* sickness. It should be *all day* sickness. I'd give anything to just have this feeling in the morning."

They reached the door, and she opened it with her key. She set her bag down and turned to JP who was still standing in the doorway.

"Melodi, I need to ask you some questions."

She looked at him directly for the first time. "You're that PI. I should've known you weren't just a nice guy helping me with my groceries."

"I just need a minute."

"If I answer your questions, will you go away and leave me alone?"

"Yes," JP said, hoping he could keep his word.

"I only have a few minutes. My husband will be home soon, and he does not need to hear any more about this."

"I'll be quick." JP delved right in. "Why did you leave Stadler?"

"Because he's a pervert who likes little girls."

"Did you tell the social worker that?"

"No. I lied because I didn't want Paige's father to know. Not that it did any good because after she left, he kept after me until I told him the truth."

"How did he take it?"

"Not well."

"Where were you Friday night around eleven o'clock?"

"I was working. I had the late-night shift tagging new merchandise that came in."

"Where was your husband?"

She hesitated. "He was working on a fishing boat. Why are you asking?"

"Because Ritchie Stadler was murdered."

JP watched the expression on her face. She looked tense, then she took a breath and sighed. He wasn't sure if the tension was because she already knew. Was she worried she or her husband would be caught? Maybe Melodi was glad the man was dead and trying to suppress her joy.

"Good," she said matter-of-factly. "I'm glad. But if you're suggesting either of us did it, you're on the wrong trail." She reached for her other bag. "You have to go. Wayne will be home any time now. It wouldn't be good for you to be here."

JP gave her the bag of groceries. "Thank you, ma'am. I appreciate your help."

As he reached the bottom of the steps, he saw a big, burly man come around the corner, carrying a six-pack of beer and holding the hand of a frail, young girl of no more than ten. The man was a few inches taller than JP and had a full beard. He was a strange contrast to the young girl. A strong, fishy smell permeated the air as they passed. JP stopped and watched as they climbed the stairs and went inside Melodi's apartment. *That must be her husband Wayne with her daughter Paige.*

JP called his friend Vinny DuBois to see if he could meet for a drink. Within twenty minutes, they were sitting inside a small bar on University, each with a beer.

"Nice to see you, McCloud."

"You too, Vinny. I see you're still on the force." His cop friend was always talking about retiring but never did. He wondered if he ever would.

"I figure one more year."

"You said that last year."

"This time I mean it."

"You said that last year too."

DuBois made a dismissive gesture with his hand. "What can I do for you?"

"I have a case I'm working for Sabre. She represents the father. The stepfather molested his little girl, and now he's dead."

"And the father is a suspect?"

"He's been questioned, but not charged, and there are plenty of other victims to choose from. But I wouldn't be surprised if something doesn't come down soon. I need to stay on top of it."

"You don't think the father killed him?"

"My gut says no, but I don't know what evidence they have, if any. Heck, I'm not even sure he's a suspect. Of course, they've questioned him, but you know how these things go. They always look close to home first."

"Who's the lead detective?" DuBois asked.

"Barry Wells."

"He's a good guy. Young, but good at his job. What he lacks in experience, he makes up for in hard work."

"Good to know."

"You'll get along with him well. He's a cowboy, like you. He even wears the boots, but not the hat."

"Yeah, I met him briefly. I noticed the boots."

DuBois chuckled.

"What's so funny?"

"Barry started his law enforcement career in a small town in Arizona, and they used to pull a lot of pranks on each other. When he came here, he tried it, but it didn't go over so well."

"So, he quit with the pranks?"

"No. He's just more careful so he doesn't get caught. His favorite stunt is buying old dolls at thrift stores and tying them on the bumpers of squad cars, especially when there's a new kid."

JP shook his head, but he admired the man's guts. "Sounds like he got thrown off the bronc a few too many times."

"True enough," DuBois said. "I know you wouldn't ask me to dig up information you're not privy to, so what do you want?"

"A more formal introduction to Wells at the least, an endorsement if you're comfortable with it. I met him, but it was brief, and a good word from you could go a long way."

"Of course. He'll work with you, especially if you have a little *quid pro quo*."

"I may be able to do that. I've been looking in places that homicide may not be aware of. Mostly, I've concentrated on the molestation, but Stadler was a financial planner who made a lot of money in some sleazy ways, so there's no shortage of possible perps."

"Call me in the morning. I'll see if I can connect you two tomorrow."

"Thanks."

"It's always a pleasure, McCloud. Thanks for the beer."

Chapter 26

Chapter 26

Monday morning

Promptly at seven, JP called DuBois, knowing he'd be in his office and answering his phone. They set up a meeting with Barry Wells, the detective on the Stadler case, for nine. After that, he had a second meeting set up with Katherine Jackson at eleven. He hoped she wasn't involved, but he had to go where the motive sent him.

While JP waited to see Wells, he started a background check on Wayne Akroyd, Melodi's husband. Thelma was right. It was no surprise to find Akroyd had a criminal background, although it had been seven years since his prison time. He'd spent three years in Donovan for an assault and battery, which had started with a fight at Qualcomm Stadium during a Chargers/Raiders game. Seventy-thousand spectators had watched on the monitor as Wayne, wearing a Raiders shirt, pummeled a guy with a blue-and-gold painted face for pouring a beer over his head. The guy claimed he'd spilled the beer, but plenty of witnesses had claimed otherwise. Wayne, however, hadn't known when to stop and nearly killed the guy. Apparently, Wayne had a temper.

JP was deep into his research when Sabre walked in, followed by Louie. Sabre said, "I'm leaving for work. Conner is taking Dené to school, and I'm dropping Morgan off, so you're on your own. Oh, and Conner took Louie out, so he's good." She leaned down and kissed him.

"Bye, sweetheart. Be safe out there."

"Always."

"Sure, honey," JP said, remembering all the times Sabre had been at risk because of her job and the chances she took.

He turned his attention back to the Akroyds and found that Melodi was Wayne's second wife. He was born in Kentucky, came to California with the Navy, and remained in the state after his discharge. He got a job operating a fishing boat until he went to prison. After his release, he returned to the same employer, working at the docks mostly, sometimes on the boats, but he could no longer operate a vessel because of his record. *That explained the fish smell when they'd passed at the apartment complex.*

Wayne's only other crimes were traffic in nature. He had one speeding ticket and another for running a red light. Melodi, on the other hand, had no traffic violations or criminal record. She was a San Diego native, graduated from Herbert Hoover High School, and married Akroyd two months after graduation. He was eleven years her senior. She gave birth to Paige three months later.

JP checked the time and decided to leave for his meeting with Wells. He'd be a little early but that was his pattern. If he wasn't fifteen minutes early, he felt like he was late.

~~~

DuBois and JP walked into the interview room and took a seat. Barry Wells entered about three minutes later.

"I understand you two have already met," DuBois said.

"Yes." Both men acknowledged. JP stood and shook his hand.

"McCloud is the guy I told you about," DuBois said. "He's a private investigator now, but he used to be one of us before he went to the dark side. We worked together for a number
~~~

of years, and we've remained friends. He's a straight-shooter and you can trust he'll do what he says. I'll see you two later."

"Thanks, Vinny." JP turned to Wells as DuBois left. "The name's JP. That man will never stop calling me McCloud."

"I understand. I had that nickname myself at my last gig. That's why I stopped wearing the hat. I refuse to give up the boots though."

JP laughed. "I don't blame you there." JP noticed the odd calluses on Wells' right hand. "Do you mind my asking, but were you a bronc rider?"

"How did you know?"

"The boots, the calluses on your right hand. I'm from Texas. I've seen plenty of those calluses. They don't come from chopping wood."

"I grew up in Fort Huachuca, Arizona. My dad was a rodeo champion. I traveled with him on the circuit riding bulls and broncs."

"Was your dad Bandy Wells, by any chance?"

Wells nodded and looked proud. "I take it you've heard of him?"

"Everybody in Texas knows about Bandy Wells. The craziest bull rider of his time."

"He was indeed."

"I guess you chose not to follow in your dad's footsteps."

"I enjoyed it when I was a kid, but I've always wanted to be in law enforcement. After high school, I was too young to get on the force, so I joined the Army. I spent most of my six years in the Middle East. And now, here I am. So, how can we help each other?"

JP explained that he worked for Sabre and the gist of the case.

"That makes the perpetrator in your case the victim in mine, correct?" Wells said.

"Right, although it's hard to think of Stadler as a victim."

"You realize your client is a person of interest to us and could become a suspect?" He tapped his calloused fingers on the table. "Because right now, he's the one we like most for the murder."

"I figured. But you need to know there are a lot of better possibilities out there."

"Such as?"

"I expect you're aware that Stadler was not only a sexual predator, he also ruined a lot of people's lives with risky financial advice."

"We know he had a bad reputation, and we're certainly looking into it. Do you have any specifics?"

"There was an older gentleman who threatened him because he lost his money. He went to Stadler's office and waved a gun in his face. Security got there before any harm was done. I don't know that it was ever reported. The company wanted it kept quiet. They thought it would be bad for business."

"Do you have a name?"

"Uri Moss, a retired flight instructor."

"Did Stadler commit fraud?" Wells asked as he wrote the name down in his file.

"I don't know for sure. Apparently, Uri couldn't afford to fight it, so the case never went to court. From what I've heard, Stadler made investments that were profitable for him, regardless of whether they benefited his clients. He also convinced Uri Moss to do a reverse mortgage and used that money as well, which left the couple in even worse shape."

"And you know all this how?"

"I spoke with an ex-colleague of Stadler's. She was actually in the room when Uri came in with the gun. I can give you her name and phone number."

"I'd appreciate that. Did you follow up on Uri Moss?"

"No. At the time, I was only interested in getting information about Stadler's sexual assault crimes."

"I take it you found others besides your client's daughter?"

"Far too many. His pattern was to date women with a young daughter, get them to move in, and then molest the child. He did that at least five times. And there could be other children he had access to over the years who didn't fit that pattern."

"Can you share those names? We'll find out eventually, but it would save me a lot of legwork and maybe get your client's name cleared sooner."

"Right now, I'm willing to give you the most likely candidate. The others I tracked are from quite a while ago. It's hard to imagine they would suddenly decide to go after him years later. I'm building trust with them, and my concern is that if you get involved, I won't get any more information. If I find out anything concrete, I'll let you know."

"I'll take whatever you're willing to share or can legally provide."

"The woman who lived with Stadler prior to his wife, Heidi, who is our client's ex-wife, is Melodi Akroyd. Her daughter, Paige, was about six or seven at the time, and her father was in prison when Melodi and Paige lived with Stadler. The father is no longer in prison and just recently found out about the abuse."

"Which would explain why he might have gone after him now."

"Exactly." JP gave him the Akroyds' address and other details he'd gathered earlier. "The wife claims they were both working. I haven't had a chance to follow up on that yet."

"Thank you. I'll let you know what I find out. We had the name Melodi, but no information yet about the husband. So, what can I do for you?"

"Do you have any physical evidence you can share with me?"

"We know the cause of death was due to a blow to the head with a hard object. The ME could tell that from the indention. We know the weapon wasn't smooth because at least the part that connected with his head appeared to be decorative. Or it could have been some kind of tool, but not like a hammer. That would leave a different kind of wound."

"So, you don't have the murder weapon?"

"We couldn't find anything in the house that matched. So, either the killer brought it with him and kept it, or found something in the house, used it, and took it with him. The wife wasn't aware of anything missing from the house."

"Burglary has been ruled out?"

"Not entirely. The killer might've come there with that intent, then had to leave before he stole anything. There was one room in the house that was torn up."

"Maybe they were looking for something in particular."

"Or it was personal. We're leaning toward the latter."

"Because?"

"One, there was no sign of forced entry, so it was likely someone Stadler knew. The word *devil* was written across the mirror. Also, whoever did this practically destroyed his train room and nothing else. Trains were strewn about the room, many of them demolished. We figure it's because Stadler was attached to his model trains. He certainly put a lot of time, effort, and money into his display. He had villages with little houses and all the trimmings. Many of the trains ran through neighborhoods or scenic areas. The lighting was odd too. It was very dim, except several of the pieces had bright red lights shining on them, making them look as if they were on fire."

"Could a boxcar from the train be the murder weapon?" JP asked.

"Possibly. But we can't tell for sure without the boxcar. We've checked them all for residue, but found nothing. The perp may have taken it with him. We don't know if anything is even missing from that room. We asked Heidi about it, but she didn't know. She almost never went in there. Mr. Chucas,

Dakota's attorney, talked to her about it, but she just said she hated that room."

"I wonder why," JP muttered.

"I can only imagine. The attorney didn't question her further because it obviously made her uncomfortable. The therapist will deal with it in time, but that may not help us."

JP thought about Belle's referring to Stadler as the "model train freak," and Katherine said she wanted to "destroy everything, including his model train room." He considered telling Wells, but changed his mind. "Do you have the time of death?"

"Between eleven and two, probably closer to eleven."

"Have you collected any DNA or fingerprints that point to the killer?"

"Not yet, or we would've likely made an arrest."

JP considered telling Wells about Uncle Tyler, but decided it might just bring them closer to Grady. The detective might even think Grady and Tyler had worked together, or that Grady had asked Tyler to do it for him. So, sharing that lead was not in the best interest of Sabre's client.

Chapter 27

Monday late morning

JP sat next to Katherine on the park bench. It was a beautiful morning. The sun was shining, and the temperature was about seventy-three degrees.

"Nice day, huh?"

"I love this time of year."

"Me too," JP said.

"But we're not here to talk about the weather," Katherine said. "What is it?"

JP was hesitant to ask some of the questions he needed to ask. He didn't want Katherine to be *the one.*

"Did Stadler hurt someone else?" Katherine asked.

"No. He was murdered a couple of nights ago."

A quick look of pain, or maybe it was confusion, passed over her face. Before she could respond, JP said, "I take it you hadn't heard about it?"

"No. How would I?"

"Thelma, maybe."

"I haven't talked to her since she told me about you." Katherine reflected. "I can't say I'm sad about Stadler dying. The whole idea of anyone getting murdered is a little unsettling, but ..."

"But it couldn't have happened to a better candidate?"

"Exactly." She paused. "You came here to tell me that? You could've done it on the phone."

"I wanted to ask you a few other questions."

"Like where was I when it happened?"

She was sharp. "I guess so. Or anything else you might know about it."

"When was he killed?"

"Friday night between eleven pm and two in the morning."

"I was home asleep."

"Was anyone else there?"

"No. My daughter had a sleepover with a friend. She doesn't do that very often. It's only been recently that I've allowed her to be away at night, except at her grandmother's. I never trusted she would be safe. I guess it's a little unfair, but I suspect everyone in the male species until they prove me wrong."

"I can understand that."

"How was he killed?"

"He took a fatal blow to the head with what appears to be a heavy object—something decorative, not smooth."

"Like a piece of art perhaps?" She spoke without emotion. "You think I used his own statue to kill him?"

"I'm not accusing, just asking."

"I can't say I haven't thought about it many times. More so in the early years. As I told you before, when I took the statue, that's exactly what I had in mind, but that urge faded over time. I'm not even sure I still have it." She shifted on the bench next to him. "I thought I put it up in the attic, but I looked for it after our visit, and I couldn't find it. Maybe I put it in a box for the thrift store. Someone may have picked up an expensive piece of art and doesn't know it."

That's convenient, JP thought. Katherine sounded convincing and a little emotionally detached. Maybe because she had actually gotten past the events, or maybe she was just too bitter to care. JP wanted to ask more about the statue, but if she hadn't used it, maybe someone close to her, like her daughter, had. He didn't dare go there or he risked losing any communication with Katherine. She was a bear when it came to protecting her cub.

"Is there anyone you can think of who might feel the need to protect you and/or your daughter?"

"No one knew about what happened except Opal and me. I never told anyone. I'm sure Opal didn't either. Other than her therapist, that is."

"Do you mind giving me the name of the therapist?"

Katherine gave him an odd look.

"I won't talk to her about Opal's case. I assume it was a woman, right?"

"Yes."

"I just want to find out if there's anything unusual in her background."

"Valerie Ellison. Her office was on Camino Del Rio North, but that was years ago. I don't know if she's still in the area or still practicing."

"Approximately how old would she be?"

"She was about thirty then, so I'd say early forties. She's African-American, and a registered child therapist."

"Thanks. I'll look into her," JP said. "What about Opal's father? Could he have found out some way?"

"No. I haven't seen him since I told him I was pregnant. He ran and never looked back. I've never had any contact with him or his family. There's no way he would even care."

"If you think of anyone else who might have wanted Stadler dead, please let me know."

"You mean like anyone who ever met him?"

JP left, not knowing much more than when he came, except that the statue was missing. He hoped it didn't mean anything. This was information he would not share with Wells, unless he had to protect Grady.

Chapter 28

Monday early afternoon

Bob and Ron checked into the facility where Carla was staying. They followed a man who led them to a patio.

"I'll be right back with Carla," the attendant said.

Ron paced back and forth along the walkway.

"Don't be nervous," Bob said. "You'll do fine."

"Thanks for setting this up," Ron said. "I take it she was okay with seeing me."

"Almost too eager," Bob said. "Her face lit up, and she never stopped smiling through the rest of our conversation. And it wasn't a creepy, 'let me at him, so I can kill him' kind of smile. She seemed to genuinely want time with you."

"Why?"

"She kept referring to it as a 'date' no matter how many times I corrected her."

They stopped talking when Carla arrived.

"Hi, Carla," Ron said as he approached, stopping a few feet before he reached her.

"Hi, Ron." Carla stepped forward, leaned in, and hugged him. She didn't let go.

Ron finally had to pry her loose.

"Sorry. It's just been so long."

"Yes, it has." Ron was eager to delve into the paternity issue, but he knew he had to make some small talk. "How are you feeling?"

"Good, now. I'm back on my medication. It helps, but it makes me feel so tired."

"It's important that you stay on your meds, especially now that you have a child."

For a split second, she glared at Ron, then just as quickly formed a smile.

Ron was struggling with what to say next, so he asked almost the same question again. "How have you been these last years?"

"Good, for the most part. Parenting has been a challenge, but my sister has been there for me." Carla stopped and looked him straight in the eyes. Her voice became very serious. "It should've been you there helping me. Liberty needs her father." Then the smile returned. "But you're here now. That's what counts."

"Carla, why do you think I'm the father?"

"Because the paternity test says so. Didn't you see it?"

"I did. But there must be a mistake."

"There's no mistake. You're the father."

"How can I be? I haven't seen you in eight years. Liberty is only four."

Carla looked at Bob for the first time, then back at Ron, and winked. "I guess God wanted it that way."

Ron decided to call her bluff. If she had tampered with the test somehow, she might be unwilling to have a second one done. "I'm thinking about getting a second test with a different lab. Do you have any objection?"

"No. It'll come out the same, but if that makes you happy, it makes me happy."

"Carla, you and I both know I'm not Liberty's father, right?"

She laughed. "You were always a jokester. I miss that." Carla shifted in her seat and started to rock back and forth.

Ron gave a nervous smile. He was getting nowhere, and Carla was getting anxious. He looked at Bob, who seemed to notice it too.

"We'd better get going," Bob said. "You look tired, Carla, and we have some other things to do."

Carla glanced at Bob again. "Okay. But when is our next date?"

"I'll see you soon," Bob said.

"I mean with Ron. You don't have to come next time if you don't want."

"We'll see," Bob said.

When they stood to leave, Ron tried to get away without a hug, but Carla grabbed him. This time was worse than the first. It took both him and Bob to get her to let go.

"See you soon, my darling," Carla said as they walked out.

"Let's go," Bob said. He added "darling" once they were out of earshot.

"That didn't go so well," Ron said.

"She's pretty adamant that you're the father."

"Because God wants it that way."

"There's that and the little thing called a paternity test."

"JP's working on it. There has to be a mistake, or someone deliberately tampered with it."

"Sure, baby daddy."

Ron glared at him.

Bob raised his hands palms up. "I'm just kidding. I'm sure JP will find out what happened."

Chapter 29

Monday afternoon

JP entered the clinic where Ron's blood had been tested, and the receptionist directed him to Quade Fuller, the fifty-something manager.

"I have some procedural questions for a juvenile court case I'm working on." JP handed him a copy of Ron's DNA results.

"I'll answer them if I can," Quade replied.

"What happens once the DNA specimen is retrieved? Where does it go? Who handles it?"

"The specimen is retrieved by one of us, so we can confirm identity of the people being tested. Since it's for legal purposes, every step of the process has to be recorded to establish chain of custody."

"And was that done in this case?"

Quade turned to his computer and made a few entries. "The saliva for the father was retrieved by technician #27345, sealed, labeled, and personally passed on to #45876. The child's DNA was obtained by technician #28704 on a different day, sealed, labeled, and passed to #47778. Both samples were checked by me to make sure they were sealed and labeled correctly. Then they went to the lab to be analyzed. Everyone who touches the samples records the chain of custody."

"Hypothetically, is there anywhere along the line where the test could either be tampered with or an error made to produce an invalid outcome?"

"Sure. Hypothetically. The sample could've been contaminated when a tube was left open, or maybe it spilled and someone tried to put it back. Or the technician didn't wear gloves and touched the sample or somehow got their own DNA in the sample."

"Does that ever happen?"

"No," The manager shook his head. "I do not know of a single case of that happening here at this clinic or any other I've worked at. But, hypothetically, it could happen."

"I get your point," JP said.

"Here's the problem with your hypothetical," Quade explained. "If the specimen was contaminated, it wouldn't show a positive paternity result unless the person who contaminated it was actually the father. If he was shown not to be the father, you'd have a better chance at that possibility, but not the other way around. Most likely it would show that the test was invalid because it had an odd mixture. But it would definitely not name him as the father." Quade took a deep breath. "The sample would have to be completely switched and there's no evidence that was done. Also, it would be very difficult."

"Could a technician have brought in a sample and switched test tubes?"

"No. The labels are generated with a sequential number and daily color."

"So, it's impossible to get the label ahead of time?"

"That's right." He scowled. "Why would someone do that?"

"Money, maybe."

"That's possible, but it doesn't sound very likely."

"What about the lab? Where could things go wrong there?"

"Same thing. If there was contamination, you would've gotten a different result."

"Does a person read the markers on the test? Could they make a mistake?"

"It's all done by computer, and the numbers are generated based on the information obtained from the DNA."

"Could they be manually changed?"

"I don't believe so. At least not by an ordinary technician. Maybe a hacker could do it, but you're really going out on a limb there."

"Here's the thing," JP said. "This man and woman once had a relationship, but it was years ago. He claims he did not have sex with the child's mother in the last eight years. The child is only four years old. Yet, the paternity test says he's the father. In fact, the father was in the witness protection program during that time. No one, including the mother, knew where he was. The man is a stable, trustworthy person I've known for years. I have no doubt he's telling the truth."

"Then there's only one explanation."

"What's that?"

"His sperm was obtained somehow and implanted in the mother."

JP thanked Quade and left the room.

JP was not far from Ron's house, so he called to meet him, and to make sure his mother wasn't there so they could speak in private. Upon confirmation, he drove directly to see Ron. They sat in the backyard under the pergola.

"I'm assuming you had a normal sexual relationship with Carla when the two of you were dating, right?" JP asked.

"Right."

"I know this is a little crazy, but could she have taken your sperm after sex, froze it, and somehow used it later? I mean could that even work?"

Ron shook his head. "I suppose, she could've done that, and theoretically it could work. But I've done some research since this all came up, and a home freezer wouldn't be adequate to do that. It needs to take place in a laboratory with proper control. Sperm needs to be kept frozen at minus one hundred ninety-six degrees centigrade. Home freezers are about minus sixteen degrees."

"That would be a hard fight with a short stick," JP said. He scratched his head. "I know this is crazy, but did you ever donate to a sperm bank?"

Ron's face turned white. "Damn! I forgot about that."

"Give me the details. Do you remember where? How many times? When exactly?"

"But how could Carla get it? How would she even know about it?"

"Back up. Just tell me when and where."

"I was in college. Some friends and I were planning a party and we needed funds. One guy suggested we sell our sperm for quick cash. He said he did it all the time. Six of us went there, and we each got seventy dollars the day we donated. We were supposed to get another thirty when it was used. Several of the guys eventually got checks, but I never did."

"Do you know the name of the clinic?"

Ron shook his head. "But I'll see if I can find out. One of the guys might remember."

"How about the location? Do you remember where it was?"

"I didn't drive, so I didn't pay attention to where it was. I remember we went there twice. We had to fill out some forms, get a physical exam, and give an initial deposit for screening. Then we went back about a week or so later to make the deposit."

"Were you dating Carla when you made your donation?"

"No. It had to have been at least two months later that I met her."

"How did you meet her?"

"She hung out in the same coffee shop we frequented."

"You're sure you never told her about the sperm bank?"

"I'm positive. I never told anyone."

"Did you do it more than once?"

"No." Ron made a strange chuckle. "I didn't want to discover someday that I had dozens of kids running around."

"You can bury that wish in a Mason jar."

"It still doesn't make sense. How could Carla end up with my sperm years later?"

"I don't know, but I aim to find out."

Chapter 30

Monday afternoon

JP went back to his home office to do some more internet research. The kids were still at school and they all had after school activities, so they wouldn't start arriving home for another hour. He had time to enjoy the peace and quiet and get some work done before then. When Louie greeted him at the door, JP got down on one knee and scratched behind his ears. When he stopped scratching, Louie bounced around, begging for more.

"That's enough, Louie. I have work to do."

JP settled in at his desk. He didn't know where to go next with Ron's problem. Besides, it had happened five years ago and wasn't going to change now. He decided to concentrate on the Harn case.

He started with a google search for Valerie Ellison, Opal's therapist. He found the name listed from California to North Carolina. There was a hair stylist in northern California and a manager of Texas Health and Human Services in Austin. He ran the name followed by RPT, but got nothing. Thirteen names popped up when he did a search on Facebook. Based on race, he eliminated all but two. One was too young. The other lived in Napavine, Washington, but showed no work history.

He searched obituaries next, but found none that matched. Most of the deceased had been far too old. He then tried

Twitter, Instagram, and LinkedIn. None had Valerie Ellison, RPT, but he did find one who looked promising in Washington D.C. Upon further research, he discovered it couldn't be her because the woman was in law school during the time Opal would've been her client.

He finally decided to drive to the location Katherine had described. Maybe the therapist was still there. It was a long-shot, but he was stuck.

He walked into the lobby and looked around for a receptionist desk. He found none, but a board near the elevators listed the various businesses and their suite numbers. No Valeries on the first floor or the second. The third had a therapist named Valerie Carter. *Perhaps she'd married and changed her last name.* JP took the elevator to the third floor. Still finding no receptionist, he walked down the hallway to Suite 312. Four names were listed, all with credentials indicating some sort of therapy degree.

Once inside, a receptionist greeted him. JP approached the desk. "I'm looking for Valerie Ellison. Do I have the right place?"

"Yes. But you're a little old for her services," the young woman said.

"I'm not here for therapy. Is she in?"

"She's gone for the day. Can I give her a message?"

JP left his card, but no message. He didn't expect to get a call. Besides, he had the information he needed for now—a name so he could check her background.

~~~

Back in his office, he ran criminal checks on Valerie using both last names, but came up empty. He ran another Google search and discovered something a little odd in her history. An issue had been brought up before the Board of Behavioral Sciences (BBS), the California state regulatory agency responsible for licensing, examination, and enforcement of
~~~

professional standards. It took some work to find out what the complaints were about.

Two different people had complained about Valerie's conduct regarding molesters. One was a comment she'd made about a child's father, the alleged molester. Normally, no one would complain about such a thing, but this mother had been convinced that her husband had done nothing wrong and hadn't liked Valerie's assessment of the situation. The other came from a co-worker who found it in bad taste when Valerie proposed, supposedly in jest, that instead of going to trial, these guys should have razor blades tied around their penises and be shown naked pictures of little girls. If the photos excited them, it would determine validity to the charges and carry out the sentence at the same time.

JP had to chuckle. He agreed with her. It sounded like Texas justice to him.

He added the therapist as another suspect to his list. He wanted to hand her name over to Wells, but then he would have to give up Katherine too. He wasn't ready to do that yet. He'd think about it. Instead, he called Valerie's office and set up an appointment to see her on Wednesday. She was reluctant at first, but agreed to give him ten minutes.

Chapter 31

Chapter 31

Tuesday morning

Sabre met Ron outside the courthouse. They sat on a bench to talk before going inside.

"So, what happens now?" Ron asked, sounding dejected.

"We go to court and question paternity. The judge will respond as if we're a little crazy. If she makes a ruling that you're the father, we'll deny the petition and set a jurisdiction trial. If she lets us have a hearing on paternity issues, we'll set a date and hope we have more information by that time."

"I'm glad you're with me, Sis."

"I wouldn't be anywhere else." Sabre sighed. "Have you thought about what you'll do if we discover she used your sperm?"

"Do I have a choice?"

"You'd still be the father of that little girl, but you likely wouldn't have legal obligations."

"I'm torn. I keep hoping we'll find a way to show it's all a mistake, even though it's looking less and less like that." He was silent for a moment. "I have to admit, I get a little excited about the thought of having a daughter. But then reality sets in. I'm not really in a position to raise a child."

"You know I will help you if that's what you decide to do."

"Thanks. But you have enough on your plate. You certainly don't need another child to help take care of." He shook his head. "It wouldn't be easy co-parenting with Carla. It's not even her issues that bother me. It's her obsession with me. I don't think she's capable of the boundaries we'd need. Reality comes and goes with her. I guess I don't know what I'll do. Take it one day at a time, I suppose."

~~~

Carla and her sister were waiting for Bob when he came out of the attorney's lounge. When Carla started asking questions, Emma nudged her, and Carla made formal introductions.

"Nice to meet you," Bob said. "How's Liberty doing?"

"Much better now that Roger and I are back," Emma said. "We never would've left if we had known this might happen. Carla was doing so well for so long."

"Where's Ron?" Carla cut in.

"He'll be here soon." Bob turned back to Emma. "The social worker says Liberty is thriving in your care."

"That's her home. We're her family."

Bob pivoted to Carla. "Are you abiding by the rules the social worker set up?"

"I am. I moved back to my apartment yesterday evening. And I'll only visit Liberty when Emma says I can."

"Carla's been very good so far." Emma patted her sister's arm. "We won't keep her from seeing her daughter. We just want Liberty to be safe."

"Where's Ron?" Carla asked again, a little louder this time.

Bob put a hand on Carla's shoulder. "Let's take a little walk." When her sister didn't move, Bob said, "You too, Emma." Bob led them to the stairs and up to the mezzanine. They sat in a cluster of chairs against the four-foot wall. Standing, you could see people in the lobby and just outside the front door, and Bob didn't want her to see Ron yet.

"Carla," Bob asked, "how did you get pregnant?"

"That's a silly question. The same way everyone does. Your momma better tell you about the birds and the bees."
~~~

"I guess it's probably time for that talk."

Carla stood and looked over the wall. "There's Ron!" She pointed to the front door. "There's my husband."

"Your what?" Bob and Emma said at the same time.

Carla was already headed toward the stairs.

"Carla, wait!" Bob called as he took off after her with Emma close behind. "He's talking to his attorney right now. We need to leave him alone."

"No. That's Sabre, his sister." Carla had reached the landing of the first set of steps.

"She's also his attorney." Bob caught up to her. "Let's give them a few minutes, then I'll go get him."

Carla kept going.

"Carla! Stop!"

"I need to talk to him."

Bob caught up to her again and explained that Ron needed time with his attorney.

A pained look crossed her face. "Okay. But I'm waiting in the lobby."

Bob and Emma followed her out the stairwell door, then stood where they could see Ron and Sabre.

"Why did you call Ron your husband?" Bob asked.

"Because we got married yesterday." She gave Bob a puzzled look. "You were there. Don't you remember?"

Emma cleared her throat. "Carla has been agitated this morning and a little confused."

"Has Carla always claimed Ron is the father of her baby?" Bob asked.

"She mentioned it once when she was stable, but she didn't want anyone to know, so I kept her secret."

"Did you know Ron was in Witness Protection when she got pregnant?"

"I didn't at the time, but that would make sense why she didn't want to tell anyone."

"He claims he never saw her."

"Yet, the test tells a different story."

Bob didn't want to say anything about the sperm bank. That was Ron's business. His client claimed Ron was the father, and the test backed it up. That's all Bob needed to know for now.

"God." Carla said, as if she were answering a question.

"What about God?"

"God is the reason Ron's the father." Carla's voice was calm. Then she opened her mouth and yelled, "Where's my husband?"

"Calm down. I'll go get him."

Carla started to follow Bob as he stepped away.

"You wait here, please."

Emma took Carla by the arm. "Stay here, honey. He'll be back in a minute."

~~~

Outside the courthouse, Ron and Sabre were still talking. "I told Lana about the paternity test coming back positive," Ron said.

"What did she say?" Sabre asked.

"She believes me. Lana hacked into the testing facility and checked on the chain of custody. She came up with the same thing JP did. The paper trail looked in order."

"The most likely scenario is that she somehow got your sperm from the sperm bank. I don't know how, but that has to be it."

"I can't imagine how she could've done that."

"Tell me something, Bro."

"What?"

She hesitated for a minute not quite sure how to broach the subject. "You and Carla seemed good together. What happened?"

"You know what happened. Witness protection sent me away."

"Why didn't you take her with you?"
~~~

"The truth is she wanted more from the relationship than I did. She always wanted marriage and children."

"And you didn't?"

"I did, but I wasn't ready. She seemed okay with putting it off for a while until just before I had to leave. We had a big fight because I discovered she stopped taking her birth control pills and that was the final straw for me."

"She always seemed so normal back then, but of course, I only saw her in small doses."

"She was very different than she is today. She was very possessive and that was a little hard to live with, but she was also loving and kind."

Sabre stood. "We'd better go in and see if we can get this done."

They walked toward the courthouse door but stopped when Bob burst through.

"You don't want to go in there just yet," he warned.

"What's going on?" Sabre asked.

"Carla saw you, and she's flipping out."

"What happened?" Ron asked.

"She said she wants her husband." Bob looked at Ron with an impish expression. "That would be you."

"Her husband?"

"Yes. I told her you were going to be here because she kept asking for you, and I thought it might calm her down, but it did just the opposite."

"Her husband?" Ron asked again.

"She said you guys got married yesterday. I guess we shouldn't have gone to see her, because the meeting went from a visit to a date to a wedding in her mind."

"Let's do this," Ron said. "Maybe I can calm her down."

"Good luck with that." Bob grinned, then turned to Sabre. "You're right. Having family in court is a bit of a nightmare—isn't it cool?"

Chapter 32

Chapter 32

Tuesday morning

Sabre, Bob, and Ron stepped inside juvenile court. The attorneys who worked there every day didn't have to go through the detector, so Sabre and Bob walked around as Ron started through.

"Good morning, Jerry," Sabre said to the marshal.

Before he could answer, Carla charged up and grabbed Ron while he was being scanned. The marshal tried to stop her, but she had already stepped inside the detector area.

"Ma'am, step out here."

"I'm sorry, sir," Ron said.

Jerry held up one arm outstretched, pointed at Ron, and snapped, "Just wait there." Two other marshals came running, and the marshal behind the detector stopped everyone else from coming through. The other men in uniform stood on either side of Carla.

Sabre spoke up. "Jerry, that's my brother."

Bob grinned, nodded toward Carla, and said, "And that's my client."

"Of course, it is," Jerry mumbled.

Jerry ran the handheld metal detector over both Ron and Carla and sent them on their way.

Carla put her arm through Ron's as if nothing had happened and said, "I'm so glad you're here, honey."

Sabre watched Ron struggle. She knew he was distressed, but he didn't want to hurt Carla. The woman had meant a lot to him once, and Sabre knew he felt a little responsible for her first break from reality. Apparently, her problems were deep-rooted and had started when she was quite young. But she'd gotten much worse after he left her. Even though they had broken up when he moved to Texas, she must've held out hope. Then he'd disappeared and everyone thought he was dead. It apparently was more than Carla could take.

Sabre felt bad for the poor woman. After Carla had her breakdown and was institutionalized, Sabre had visited her a lot. In fact, she had been the only one who could calm Carla down when she acted out. The facility had called Sabre to come in or at least talk to Carla on the phone. Sabre couldn't remember how it started, but she would tell her a story about butterflies and flowers and it had soothed her.

Ron walked with Carla down the hallway, easing her arm from his. "This isn't the place, Carla."

She seemed to accept that and kept chatting as if everything was normal.

When they reached Department One, Terry Chucas, the minor's attorney, was waiting for them. "Is everyone ready?" he asked.

"Can I talk to you a minute?" Sabre stepped away from Carla.

"Sure."

They walked away so they could have some privacy. Sabre explained that Ron was her brother, and she was there to represent him.

"Good. The test says he's the father, so he'd be given counsel anyway."

"That's the problem." She explained about the test, the timing of the conception, and the sperm bank donation. "We have no idea how she got access to the sperm, but that's the only real possibility since Ron was in WITSEC."

"He was in the witness protection program?"

"Yup."

"Wow. That's a new one." Chucas took a deep breath. "I assume he doesn't want to parent the child."

"He's torn. He loves children, but he doesn't think he's ready."

"None of us ever are."

"This is all so sudden. I think he needs to live with it for a while. Setting a trial date will give us all time to figure it out. And we'll be ready to contest the petition if it comes to that."

"Does he want to see Liberty?"

"Not yet. He doesn't want to confuse her. She gets enough of that with her mother."

"I agree," Terry said. "You know, if it was anyone else, I'd just assume he was lying about the paternity. But if you believe him, I'll let you try and prove it. That would be the fair thing for Liberty."

"Thanks, Terry."

They walked back to the group. Sabre explained the hearing would be a request for a trial and gathered a couple of dates that everyone was available.

Sabre said, "I'll go in and get this on calendar as soon as we can."

"Thank you," Emma said.

Sabre went inside and explained to the bailiff that she was representing the alleged father and that the mother was a little volatile. "All the attorneys are ready on the case. I'm requesting a trial, and we've selected possible dates."

"What are they?"

Sabre gave him the dates.

"Gather the troops. You're next."

Sabre brought everyone in, they took their seats at the table, and the case was called.

"Your Honor," Sabre said as she stood. "I'm representing the alleged father, Ronald Brown."

"Any relation?" Judge Hekman asked.

"My brother."

The judge raised an eyebrow. "You're denying the petition?"

"Actually, Your Honor, we're denying the paternity. We're asking for a hearing on that issue."

"Did you see the DNA results?"

"Yes, Your Honor. However, there are extenuating circumstances that we believe do not make him the legal father."

The judge shook her head and glanced around the room at the other attorneys.

Bob stood. "Your Honor, there's physical evidence that Mr. Brown is the father of this child. My client has stated he's the father of this child. Mr. Brown can set a jurisdictional trial as the father on this case if he chooses, but I ask we move forward."

"County Counsel?" Judge Hekman asked.

"We join in mother's attorney's request."

"Mr. Chucas?"

"I join with Ms. Brown in her request. I think we need to adjudicate this issue before we go any further. If there is some inaccuracy in the test, or something else that makes this invalid, we don't want a jurisdictional trial and then place the child with someone who turns out not to be the father."

Judge Hekman looked perplexed. Finally, she said, "I don't want this to drag out any longer than it has to. We'll set a date for next Monday afternoon on the paternity issue alone, and all prior orders remain in effect."

As they all stood to leave, Carla asked, "What happened?" Bob whispered something to her, and she said loudly, "He's her father."

"Please keep your voice down." Bob pleaded.

Carla suddenly started flapping her arms and screaming, "God did it! God did it! God did it!" She gasped for breath between words.

Bob tried to calm her, but he couldn't. Emma tried. Still nothing. Several bailiffs had come in the courtroom, ready for anything, so Sabre stepped forward. "Let me try."

"Carla, it's Sabre. Please listen to me."

The woman kept screaming, and the bailiffs stepped closer.

Sabre help up a hand. "I got this."

Sabre raised her voice. "Butterflies, green pastures, and butterflies." Carla paused and looked at her. Sabre started again. "Butterflies, green pastures, and butterflies. Carla, imagine yourself walking through the field and a beautiful pink-and-purple butterfly lands on your arm."

Carla raised her arm and looked, as if the butterfly were there, still quiet.

Sabre went on. "You look around and see little dots of color—pink, purple, yellow, red. All the beautiful butterflies are landing on the green blades of grass. The tall grass is moving slightly in the light breeze, and a rainbow of multi-colored butterflies dance across the pale blue sky." Sabre struggled to remember the words she used to say, but Carla listened intently. "There's no one else in your world, just you and your butterflies, wandering through your green pasture."

Sabre took Carla by the arm and led her out of the courtroom, still talking about butterflies. Once outside, they sat down. Sabre continued talking until Carla was breathing comfortably. Then Sabre said, as she always had in the past, "Don't worry, Carla. I'll take care of everything."

Chapter 33

Tuesday morning

At Barry Wells' request, JP stopped by the police department headquarters. After getting through security, a desk officer led him to the homicide detective's cubicle.

As he walked in, Wells was retrieving a file from a cabinet. "You can strike Akroyd off your list," he said without greeting. "He was out on a fishing boat from Friday morning to Monday afternoon. They were off the shores of Mexico."

"Did they dock at any time?" JP took a seat.

"No. The only way he could've gotten back is with another boat, and several witnesses accounted for his whereabouts."

"Dang. I was afraid that was too simple. What about his wife, Melodi?"

"She was tagging new merchandise at Marshalls. She got there about nine-thirty pm and didn't leave until six the next morning. You can't leave the store without setting off the alarm, and the manager has to disarm it. She's covered."

"There's Uri Moss. What about him?"

"He's still a possibility and seems to have disappeared."

"What do you mean?"

"His neighbors said he left with a small bag on Wednesday and hasn't returned."

"Was the bag big enough to hold the murder weapon?"

"Possibly. We don't know exactly what the weapon is yet. But we know it has some sharp edges. We haven't shared this with the public, but Stadler was hit more than once. Several times in fact, maybe even after he was dead."

"So, it *was* personal."

"We think so."

"Were there cuts from the blows?"

He shook his head. "Just a lot of petechia on his face and some large bruises—one on his forehead, and several on his arms."

"That's curious."

"It is. And I don't think we'll find the murder weapon until we find the killer."

"No prints?"

"Nothing we didn't expect to find. Whoever did this must've worn gloves, which means it was premeditated. And I don't have to tell you, but your client has a strong motive. I can't say I would blame him. If my child were molested, I wouldn't take it lightly."

"Which leaves a long line of motivated people; his victims, many of whom aren't children anymore, their parents, and the financial victims and their families."

Wells nodded. "True enough."

"Sabre told me you questioned Grady again."

"We did, and he says all the right stuff. I actually like the guy. I wish he had an alibi."

"You and me both," JP said. "What about Heidi? Anything new on her? Maybe she finally figured out what a dirt bag her husband was and decided to end it."

"We confirmed she was at her mother's, but it's possible she snuck out and returned without anyone knowing. But she's a tiny thing, and doesn't appear too strong. Whoever did this needed a decent amount of upper body strength to inflict the blows he did."

"So, you think it's a man?"

"Or a *strong* woman."

"Or, an angry one with lots of adrenaline."

"Perhaps," Wells said.

"And if it was Heidi, she wouldn't need to wear gloves," JP pushed the scenario. "I'm sure you found plenty of her prints everywhere since it's her house."

"That's true. Have you learned anything new?"

"Not much," JP said. "I know you talked to Thelma, Stadler's next door neighbor."

"She told me about the person she saw and the white SUV. Other than that, she didn't have much information. She certainly wasn't very talkative."

JP found that curious since she had talked his ear off. "Did she tell you Heidi came to see her on Friday and told her she was going to her mother's?"

"No. But we already knew where Heidi was." He paused. "I wonder why Thelma didn't mention that to me."

"We've bonded. I like the old lady. She knows the difference between an ox and a whiffletree."

Wells looked confused. "I don't know what that means."

"It doesn't matter. The thing is, Heidi had never been to Thelma's house except when Dakota wanted to play in the backyard. They're not exactly friends."

"You think she was establishing an alibi?"

"It's possible. I'm not trying to point the finger at anyone. It may not be relevant."

"Thank you. It's information we didn't have before. I'll follow up on it."

~~~

JP called Katherine as soon as he left the department, and she agreed to meet him again at the coffee shop. They sat at the same table outside, and JP got right down to business. "Whoever killed Stadler did it with an unusual weapon."

"You think I did it?"

"No," JP answered quickly. "But I think the weapon may have been in your possession at one time."
~~~

"Besides me, Opal is the only person who knew about the dragon statue." Her eyes went wide. "Are you accusing Opal?"

"No."

"You would be off base there. Opal keeps things inside. I worry more about the harm she might do to herself. That's far more likely than anything she might do to anyone else. She's just not that kind of person."

"I'm not suggesting she is. I need you to think about what you might have done with that statue. Maybe I can trace it."

Katherine shook her head. "I honestly have no idea where it is. I don't remember giving it away or tossing it out. It was just with a bunch of stuff I never looked at. When I moved from the last house, I had some friends help me. The stuff that came out of my junk closet, where I kept it, went straight into the new attic. I never looked in the box. Maybe it got left behind."

"Is it possible one of them took it?"

"I can't imagine. If they wanted it, I'm sure they would've asked."

"The only other person who knew about Opal's abuse was her therapist, right?"

"Correct."

"Is there any way she could've gotten it?" JP asked. "Could Opal have given it to her?"

"That's highly unlikely."

"I know. I'm stretching for answers."

"It's possible the statue is still in the attic and I just couldn't find it. There's a lot of stuff up there. I can look again, but not today. I'm too busy. It'll have to wait until tomorrow or the next day."

"See what you can do."

"What happens if I find it? Wouldn't that just put suspicion on me or someone who knows me?" She shook her head. "I'm not going to create another problem for Opal. Forget it." She stood. "I shouldn't have come here."

"I'm sorry." JP stood too. "I'm just trying to get to the bottom of this murder."

Katherine started to leave, then stopped. "Wait a minute. There were two of those statues. Where's the other one?"

"You never said there were two."

"I had forgotten. Actually, I never saw the second one, but I remember Ritchie saying they had been a set. That the remaining statue wasn't worth as much because the other one had been stolen."

"Do you know how long it had been gone?"

"No idea."

"Did he say how it was stolen? Was he robbed?"

"I don't think so. I got the impression it was someone he knew." She gave a small smile. "Maybe she had the same idea I did when I took mine."

Chapter 34

Chapter 34

Tuesday afternoon

Ron sat at Sabre's house in front of his laptop perusing Facebook for his college friends. He had to find someone who remembered the name of the sperm bank. He tried to recall the place, but he'd put the whole thing out of his mind long ago. It bothered him that there might be "little Rons" running around out there that he didn't know about. What about Liberty? Did he want to get to know her? Did he want to help raise her? One minute he thought he did, and the next he didn't.

Sabre walked in and interrupted his thoughts. "Hey, Bro. You look pensive. What's on your mind?"

"I was just wondering how many other kids I have because of that one foolish act."

"Maybe none." She put a hand on his shoulder. "Or maybe you've provided some couple, who had given up hope, with a child they love and are giving a great home to."

"I'm surprised you can put a positive spin on it, considering the work you do. My children could be going through your court system every day, and we don't even know it."

"Come on, Ron. You only donated once, and you never got paid, right?"

"Right."

"So, your sample was never used."

"Except for Carla."

Sabre removed her hand. "That was four years later, and you still didn't get paid."

"You mean the place wasn't legit and didn't pay like it should have. So what?"

"Or the sperm bank didn't *sell* the sperm?"

"So, you're saying she must've gotten it illegally."

"Exactly."

"But how?"

"That's a question for JP to figure out. You just need to do some legwork for him. Find out the name of the clinic and any information you can get from your buddies who went with you."

"I'm having trouble even remembering their names. Except Paul, but I can't recall his last name. There was Francisco." Ron searched his brain for the last name, then tapped the air with his finger. "Ramos. Francisco Ramos. He was Filipino, and a really funny guy. The one who started it all was Zack, a friend of Paul's."

"You have a start. Maybe you can find Francisco and he'll lead you to the others."

"Maybe. I didn't know any of them that well."

"I don't remember any of those names, but you had a lot of friends I never met."

"I was afraid if I brought my friends home, they'd hit on you, and then I'd have to do the big brother thing."

"Yeah, right."

Ron thought about Liberty, a girl without a father or big brother.

"What is it?" Sabre asked.

"I don't know what to do about Liberty. The thought of raising a child with Carla is frightening. She's so obsessed with me that the whole thing would probably be harder on Liberty than not having a father at all."

"You may be right, but she has Roger. She even calls him Papa. I think she sees Roger and Emma as her parents. Don't get me wrong. I think she loves Carla, but according to the social worker, Liberty is far more comfortable with her aunt and uncle. And why wouldn't she be? They are her safe zone when her mother leaves or goes off the deep end."

"What are you saying?"

"Whatever you do, I'll support you. Liberty seems to be happy with her current situation. She has Carla who loves her, and she has stable role models and protectors in the Griffins. Upsetting that dynamic may not be in the best interest of the child. On the other hand, you have a lot to offer any child. You'll make an amazing father if that's your choice. She's young enough that she'll adjust. It'll take a little time, but I know she would ultimately be better with you in her life." Sabre paused. "Unless, as you said, Carla makes it unbearable. That would be hard on you and Liberty."

"There is no *right* choice."

"Or, maybe there is no *wrong* one. There's only the best choice you can make that you believe you can live with down the road." She leaned over, kissed him on the cheek, and started to walk away.

"Thanks, Sis. You've been a big help." His light-hearted sarcasm was obvious.

When Sabre left, Ron called Lana. "I'm in a bit of a pickle," Ron said.

"What is it?"

"I don't know what to do about Liberty. I'm confused, frustrated, and torn."

"I can't help you with that. You have to figure it out yourself."

"You're right," Ron said. "We've set the paternity issue for trial, but I don't know how to prove I didn't voluntarily create that little girl."

"Does it matter?"

"I don't know." Ron hesitated. "I do know that if I'd had sex with her to create that child, I would absolutely step up. But I didn't. I feel violated, if that makes sense. I feel like she stole something from me."

"Something you had already given away. I take that back. Something you had already sold to someone else."

That hurt a little. "Do you think I'm wrong in questioning my responsibility?"

"Not at all. I agree that what she did was offensive."

"But …?" The word hung in the air.

"Some people would feel like she was their child, no matter how she was created. That somehow the DNA is magic."

"I intentionally don't want to get to know her unless I'm committed to raising her, and I don't think I'm ready for that. Also, she has an aunt and uncle who have been parenting her more than Carla has. If they weren't in the picture, maybe I would feel differently, but they are. If Carla wasn't around, they'd gladly adopt her."

"It sounds like you've answered your first question about what to do. The only thing left is to prove it was involuntary. Then you can reassess and make a decision."

"Is that what you would do?"

"I would feel violated if someone did that with my eggs, but it doesn't matter what I would do. Thankfully, I won't have to ever make that decision."

He didn't think she was being condescending or sarcastic, but he wasn't exactly sure what she was saying. Was she saying she would never be in that spot because she would never have sold her eggs? Or was she not able to have children? What if that was the case and he ended up with Lana as a life partner? This could be his only chance to have a child. He shook his head and moved on. It was way too early to think about that.

"Thanks for listening."

"Anytime. What sperm bank did you go to?"

"I can't remember."

"If you find the name, I'd be glad to do a little inside snooping for you."

Chapter 35

Chapter 35

Tuesday afternoon

Ron searched Facebook for Francisco Ramos. The first three listed were an athlete, an artist, and a comedian. He ruled out the athlete right away because the profile pic was obviously not him. The most likely was the comedian. Francisco was always a funny guy, but Ron never knew him to have ambitions in that direction. His profile pic was a logo, so he opened his page and quickly discovered that wasn't him. The photos were obviously of a much older man. He searched further for more names.

One Francisco Ramos was in San Diego, but his page had little information and the photo featured two children. He sent a message, but since the page hadn't been updated in over a year, he didn't expect much.

Next, he tried Google. It was page after page of the comedian with the same name. Ron switched to LinkedIn and found more of them there. He scrolled through the list and found Francisco Ramos working at Salubrious Labs, a health research company, which made sense. His friend had been a business major with a science minor. As soon as Ron saw the photo, he knew it was him.

It didn't take much effort to find his work number.

"Francisco Ramos," the man said when he answered. "Can I help you?"

"This is Ron Brown. I don't know if you remember me, but we went to State together."

"Ron! Boy, is this a blast from the past. How are you? What are you doing these days?"

"I worked at Parks and Rec for a while, then I moved out of state for about five years." He didn't want to get into the whole Witness Protection thing, so he kept it short. "I'm back now and doing investigations for my sister who practices law. What about you?"

"I've been with this company since I got my doctorate. I love it here. I'm married and have two kids. Life is good."

"I'm glad to hear that," Ron said. "Speaking of kids, do you remember when we went to that sperm bank?"

"Yeah. Crazy Zack got us into that. He was a regular, but I never went back. Did you?"

"No. That wasn't for me." Ron paused. "Do you remember the name of the clinic?"

"I don't, man. Why?"

Ron explained briefly what happened.

"That's wild! I wish I could help."

"Do you know how I can find Zack, or even what his last name is?"

"No. But Paul would know his name, maybe even where he is. They were good friends. I haven't spoken to Paul in about six months, but I have his number. I'll text it after we hang up. Then you'll have my cell number too. Give me a call sometime, and we'll get together for a drink or something. I have to go now, but it was nice talking to you."

Shortly after they hung up, Ron received the text. He added Paul Kirby as a contact, then called him.

Paul was as surprised to hear from Ron as Francisco had been. They chatted about old times and caught up on each other's lives. Paul was married with a baby on the way and working for the airlines in a management position. He wasn't crazy about his job, but it paid well. Ron suddenly felt unsettled about his life. His college friends seemed on track with their dreams, their jobs, and their personal lives—while he was a bachelor in his mid-thirties with no real career path.

Ron gave him the Readers Digest version, then asked if he remembered the clinic.

"I'm sorry. I don't. I do remember about where it was though. It was on La Mesa or University, I think. No, it might have been College. It wasn't far from State; I remember that much. Zack would know for sure. He went several times a week and got residual checks like crazy even after he stopped." Paul snickered. "I think he stopped. Who knows? He may still be making deposits."

"Do you have his number?"

"I have one, if it's still good. I haven't seen or talked to him in a couple of years. We don't have much in common anymore. I was the best man at his wedding, but the marriage only lasted a year. He's basically a pot-smoking beach bum. He goes surfing every day if the waves are high enough. He was living in a small apartment in Ocean Beach the last I knew. You know Zack. He was always a little wild and different."

Paul gave him a phone number and address. "They may not be good anymore." Before they hung up, they agreed to keep in touch, but Ron didn't think it was likely they would.

Ron called and got a voicemail message, but at least it was Zack's number. He left a message, feeling more and more anxious. He hated the whole situation. It seemed so unfair, not only to him, but to everyone involved. *How could it possibly have happened?*

Ron found himself pacing and decided he couldn't just sit there. He would drive to Zack's apartment and wait if he wasn't home.

Ron knocked on the apartment number Paul had given him. A young woman answered the door. She looked like she just woke up, or maybe she was wasted. She was barefoot and dressed in a long Greta Van Fleet t-shirt with no pants.

"I'm here to see Zack."

"He's the surfer guy, with the VW van, right?"

"Yeah, that's him."

"He ain't here."

"Do you know when he'll be back?"

"No idea. He didn't give me his schedule." She yawned. "Look, I don't really know the guy. I just met him yesterday, and he said I could crash here for a while. He's like pretty cool you know." Her head swayed and her eyes were dilated. "You can come in if you want."

Ron decided against it. "Thanks, but I'll wait in my car for a little while." Ron wrote his name and number on the notepad he kept in his pocket. He tore out the sheet and gave it to her. "If I have to leave before he returns, will you please ask him to call me as soon as he can?"

"Sure." She took the paper, tugged on the top of her t-shirt, and dropped it in. The paper fell to the floor. "Oops." She picked it up.

Ron doubted Zack would get the message if he left, so he went to his car and waited. He got restless after an hour, but then a blue VW van pulled into the parking spot marked with Zack's number. Ron got out of his car and walked toward him. He caught Zack just before he reached the apartment. No longer a clean-cut college student, Zack's light-brown hair was below his shoulders and he sported a goatee.

"Zack?"

He turned around. "Yes?"

"It's Ron Brown. We went to State together. Remember me?"

"Yeah, man." He unlocked his front door. "Come on in."

Ron was relieved the girl he'd spoken to earlier was not in the living room. They sat down and caught up on the last ten years. Ron told him what he needed and asked, "Do you know the name of the sperm bank we went to?"

"I used several because they limited the number of deposits you could make per week. That was good money back then, man."

"What about the one we went to with Francisco and Paul. We needed money for a party we were having. Remember?"

"Sort of."

"This one was near the college."

"Yeah. I think that was my first." Zack tapped his forehead, as if he was trying to jog loose a memory. "Uh ... uh ... what was it called? It was just off El Cajon between College and Fifty-fourth. I can't remember the name of the street." He pushed his hair behind his right ear. "There's a Catholic church not far away. I used to pass it whenever I went." His hair fell in his face and he pushed it back again. "The clinic was about a block away around the corner." Zack took out a hair-tie and twisted his hair into a man-bun. "It's been years since I was there, not even sure it's still open. I'm sorry, man."

"That's all right. Maybe I can find it with what you gave me." Ron started toward the door. "It was nice seeing you."

"Wait," Zack said. He walked over to a cupboard and took out a box of papers. He shuffled through them and pulled out a document. "Uh huh." He gave the paper to Ron. "There's the name. It was called something else when I first started going, but I think a national company bought them out so it's probably still operating."

"Thanks." Ron sighed in relief.

"I hope it helps, man." He slapped Ron on the shoulder. "You know, I often wonder how many children I have out there."

"I do too now." Ron grimaced and left.

Chapter 36

Chapter 36

Tuesday evening

JP sat at his desk mulling over the facts on the Stadler/Harn case. He needed to find the second statue, if there actually was one. He wanted to believe Katherine, but it seemed a little too convenient to throw in another statue when he'd questioned the location of hers. But if there was a second, it had gone missing pre-Katherine. Who knew how many women had passed through Stadler's house? The only long-term stays, before Heidi, were Izzy and Belle and both of them were dead.

If the statues were valuable as Stadler had claimed, he may have had them insured, and likely reported the one stolen. Maybe even collected insurance money. *But then why wouldn't he have claimed both of them were missing?* It was a long shot, but JP called Wells and asked if Stadler ever reported a burglary or a robbery in his house.

"What does this have to do with the murder?"

"I have reason to believe that statue may be the murder weapon."

"What are you not telling me, Torn?" The detective sounded irritated.

"I'll let you know if this leads to anything. Right now, it's just a hunch."

Wells sighed. "It's a good thing DuBois vouches for you because you're starting to tick me off." Wells hung up.

JP could hear Sabre in the kitchen. He wanted to spend some time with her, but he had too many loose ends on this case. He did a quick search for Natalie Hernandez that turned out to be easier than he'd expected. She had a Facebook page where she talked about her mother's death and how the world didn't care. She also asked for anyone who might help *avenge* her death. JP thought it might be more like a cry for help in finding the killer. Her page also had information about where she worked, a small Mexican restaurant in Clairemont called Maritza's. He shook his head. The information was helpful to him, but people didn't realize how they exposed themselves to the world with their social media posts. He made a mental note to talk to Conner and Morgan, although neither spent much time on the internet. Morgan didn't have a phone, and Conner was too busy. JP still wanted them to realize the potential danger, especially since their father might have enemies they were not aware of. Dené was different. She posted on Snapchat, TikTok, and Instagram. He made a mental note to make sure Dené was involved in their discussion.

He was re-reading his notes when Sabre walked in. "It's almost time for dinner," she said.

Without responding to her comment, he said, "The first two women, that we know of, who lived with Stadler are dead, but their children, the victims, are still alive."

"You think one of them killed Stadler?"

"Just pondering. I haven't even talked to Natalie, Izzy's daughter. But I just found out where she works, so I'll pay her a visit."

"What about Belle? You've talked to her."

"She didn't strike me as the killing type. She seems to have gotten her act together and is determined to live a different life than her mother's."

"Isn't she a stripper? That doesn't sound much different."

"She has the same job, but she's not living the same life." JP remembered something and checked his notes. "She did say she had something valuable from her mother. You don't suppose it was the statue?" Sabre shrugged, and before she could respond, JP added, "She also said she had one more mess to clean up for her mother. Maybe Stadler was the mess."

"I just hope you find something soon, because the cops are putting more pressure on my client."

"They don't have any real evidence on him."

"Actually, they may have a little more now."

"What's that?"

"I found out today that Stadler left a trust which he changed just a few months ago. He was originally leaving everything he owned to some model train society."

"And now?"

"He left everything to Dakota and Farrah," Sabre said. "Evenly split."

"Nothing to his wife?"

"Just the girls, which means Grady's daughter benefits from Stadler's death."

"But that could also put more suspicion on Heidi."

"True. Or both of them together." She touched his face lovingly. "Are you going to eat with us?"

"I'm not very hungry." He stood, kissed her, and said, "I'm going out—for work. I'll see you later."

JP grabbed his keys from the hook on the wall and went out the front door. Ron was coming up the walkway and asked, "Where are you off to?"

"I need to see a potential witness," JP said. "Dinner is ready. I'm not eating so I'm sure there's plenty. Or, you can have Mexican food with me."

"Did you cook, or was it Sabre?"

"Sabre."

"Mexican food it is."

"That was cold," JP said.

"I just love Mexican food." Ron winked and turned around.

They got into JP's truck. "I hope you're not in a hurry because I also need to see Belle again."

"That's fine."

"Maybe Poodle will be there. I think she liked you."

"Just drive."

Chapter 37

Maritza's was a tiny restaurant with only ten small tables set up for inside dining, four of which were filled. JP saw several take-out orders bagged and ready under the heat lamp. Two older Latino men were working the grill behind the cutout window. A woman in her early twenties was taking orders. She wasn't stunning like Belle, but she had a natural beauty and when she smiled, her face lit up, making her more attractive.

They ordered food, paid for it with cash, as the sign instructed, and took a seat near the door.

"Do you think that's her?" Ron asked.

"We'll find out when she brings our food."

It took a while to get their meals. Six people had come in and picked up to-go orders, and the phone rang several times with new orders. Three of the tables had emptied by the time the waitress brought their dinner.

"Is the food good here?" JP asked. "This is our first time."

"It's the best in town. The salsa is like no other, except for Carmen's, where I used to work. Theirs is just as good, but it's owned by the same family."

"You can always tell a good Mexican restaurant by its salsa," Ron said. "What's your name?"

"Natalie." She set down the last plate.

"Thanks, Natalie."

"Bingo," Ron said, when she was gone.

"Take your time eating, because our only chance of talking to her is when this place clears out and she's not so busy."

An hour later, as they sipped beer and killed time, they finally got their break. Natalie walked over to see if they needed anything else.

"Can you talk a minute?" JP asked.

She looked back toward the kitchen, then said, "Sure. Watcha need?"

"Was your mother Izzy Hernandez?"

Natalie's eyes widened, then she grabbed a chair and sat down. "Yes. Did you know her?"

"We never met." JP tipped his head. "I'm so sorry for your loss and the tragic way it happened."

"Me too." She swallowed. "She had lots of problems, but she never let me forget how much she loved me."

"You're lucky for that."

"How do you know about her? Are you a cop?"

"A private investigator. JP Torn. I'm investigating the death of Ritchie Stadler."

She suddenly looked uncomfortable. "Of course—a rich, white guy."

"Do you remember him?"

"I'll never forget that model train-loving pedophile."

JP had to wonder what went on in that room. It had certainly left a bad impression on the children who'd lived there. "I'm so sorry for what you went through."

"What angers me is that they'll spend a lot of time trying to find out who killed that pedo. And his murder was probably justified. I wish people cared enough about my mother to investigate her death." She sounded more defeated than bitter.

"I do *not* care about Stadler." JP locked eyes on her. "That man is so low, he probably has to look up to see hell. I'm investigating because they're pointing the finger at our client, whose daughter was molested by Stadler."

Her eyes dropped to the floor. "He's been doing that for decades. It's about time someone stopped him."

"Well, that dog won't hunt again."

Natalie gave him an odd look. "I haven't seen Stadler since we left his mansion seventeen years ago. What do you want from me?"

"I know you were young, but do you remember some statues that sat on the tables near the front door?"

She didn't answer right away. JP wondered if she was trying to remember or deciding whether she should say anything. "I remember one. He loved that ugly thing. He was always telling us not to touch it, claimed it was worth a lot of money. Once, when he was gone, I knocked it off the table trying to break it, but it wouldn't break. I got into trouble with my mom." She sighed. "My mother wasn't using drugs back then. She wasn't hooking either. We had lost our home when Stadler took us in, but we were doing okay. After we left him, she totally lost it. Mom did anything to make money just to keep us from having to rely on some pervert. Eventually, she started using drugs. She said it made it easier to do her job. I was a teenager before she got really bad." Her eyes watered. "I miss her, and I wish they would find who killed her."

"I'm so sorry, Natalie," JP said. "There's nothing I can do right now because I'm too busy. But when I get some spare time, I'll see what I can find out for you."

"I don't have any money," she said. "I can barely make it now with what I earn. I want to go to beauty school, but I can't afford the tuition. I thought I could work and go at the same time, but part-time work only covers my living expenses. And to top that off, my clunker of a car broke down again. I don't know what that's going to cost me." She waved her hands around dismissively. "I'm sorry. You don't need to hear my troubles."

"I didn't ask for any money," JP said. "Besides, I don't know how much I'll be able to do. If the cops couldn't find anything, I may not be able to either."

"I'd appreciate it if you'd try. That's more than the cops have done."

JP knew better than that, but street murders were difficult. Witnesses, if there were any, were seldom willing to talk, and credibility was often an issue if they did. JP gave Natalie his card and told her to call him in a week or so.

She stood. "I need to get back to work."

"One more thing," JP said. "Do you mind telling me where you were Friday night?"

"Hmph." She sighed. "Is that when he was killed?"

"Yes. And you don't have to tell me, but eventually, the police will find you and it would be nice if you had a verifiable alibi."

She gave a half smile. "Actually, I do. Some friends picked me up after work. I changed clothes at home, then we went bar hopping. About two in the morning, we took an Uber to Whitney's house and crashed there. I'll gladly give you the names of the friends and the bars we went to."

"Thank you. That would be helpful."

Ron took out a notebook and jotted down the information Natalie gave them.

They stood to leave, and JP thanked her again. "I'll be in touch. And I promise I'll look into your mother's death."

Ron went to the counter, asked for napkins, and slipped a hundred-dollar bill into the tip jar.

"What was that about?"

"A Random Act of Kindness. That tip was from Aunt Goldie."

Chapter 38

Chapter 38

Tuesday night

Poodle approached Ron as soon as he and JP walked in the strip club's door. "Welcome back, stranger. Come join me."

They headed toward the bar. Belle was dancing, and a group of young men seated near the stage were whooping and hollering at her. Belle catered to them, probably because there weren't many others in the bar, and they were just drunk enough to be good tippers. It was obviously a bachelor party. One man was wearing a baseball cap that said *Groom* on it. The rest were buying him drinks.

When Belle strutted onto their table, they got even louder. JP swore he saw tongues hanging out like slobbering dogs, as their wallets opened and the bills came out. By the time she reached the end of the table, her bra and skimpy panties were filled with money. She slowly danced her way back, picking up more cash, then stopped and shoved her boobs right into the groom's face. A moment later, she was back on the stage.

JP continued to watch the action, sizing up everyone and remembering his bar days. Life was so much better now. He loved his relationship with Sabre, and he enjoyed raising his niece and nephew. Even Dené was starting to grow on him. He hoped Sabre was as happy as he was.

"Hi, Cowboy," Belle said, stopping by. She nodded at Ron, then turned back to JP. "Nice to see you. Please tell me you came for the view and not more information."

"Sorry, darlin', just doin' my job. Besides, I'm very happily involved."

"The good ones always are." She smiled. "What do you need?"

"Do you remember a couple of statues that Ritchie had by his front door?"

A strange look came over her face, and her tone seemed to change. "Yeah. I remember them. They were ugly, like Ritchie."

"How many were there?"

"One on each side of the foyer, just before you got to the door. Why?"

"We've been able to account for one of them, but the other is missing."

"I bet that burned Ritchie's butt. He loved those things."

"Do you have any idea what happened to the second one?"

"How would I?"

"I thought maybe he sold it while you were there, or that it was stolen. Do you remember anything happening to it?"

"No. I don't." She turned to the bartender. "What time is it, Tony?"

"Almost time for your next act."

"Sorry, Cowboy. I've got to go. I wish I could've been more help."

On their way out, Ron asked, "Do you think Belle killed Stadler?"

"She had motive for sure, but they all do. It may be the thing she had to do for her mother."

"But why now?"

"I don't know, but she sure acted strange when I asked about the statues."

Ron nodded. "I noticed that too."

"I'm not ready to check her off my list, but I hope it's not her."

"You've said that about every suspect so far."

"That's 'cuz no one blames you when you kill a rattlesnake."

~~~

Sabre sat on the sofa with a glass of wine. She put her feet up and relaxed for the first time. Her workday had ended around five, but then she'd cooked dinner and helped the girls clean the kitchen. They were very good about it, except when they were fighting, which seemed to be about half the time. Tonight had been one of those nights. While she'd helped Conner with his Spanish homework, she'd had to settle differences between Morgan and Dené three times. By the time she got them to bed and sat down, she was beat. She had just kicked back when JP came home.

"You look like you've been chewed up, spit out, and stepped on," JP said.

"That's a good description of how I feel."

He sat down next to her. "Are you okay, darlin'?"

"It's been a long day and a lot of frustration. And the girls are at it again."

"Too bad. They seemed to be getting along so well."

"For about three days. I think that was a record."

"What's the beef this time?"

"Apparently, some boy likes Dené, which I don't like for starters, but Morgan seems to be jealous."

"Does Morgan like him?"

"She doesn't even know him. I'm not sure if she's upset because she doesn't have anyone who likes her, or if she doesn't like that Dené is giving the boy too much attention. They're both far too young to have boy issues. I'm not ready to deal with that."

"Me either," JP said. "But we'll take it as it comes."

"And this thing with Ron is driving me mad. He is so torn up about what to do, and if I don't win the paternity trial,
~~~

he'll be on the hook financially to at least support that child. And I know he wants to do what's right by her, but he doesn't want to take her away from Aunt Emma either. And can you imagine dealing with Carla for the next fifteen or twenty years? I would love to have a niece, but I don't want to influence his decision."

"That's a smart move."

"And I had that same nightmare again last night. It's driving me a little crazy." She sighed. "I'm sorry. Did you get any closer on the Harn case?"

"Maybe." JP told her about Belle and Natalie and his suspicion that one of the statues could be the murder weapon. "Assuming Natalie is telling the truth, which I have no reason to dispute, the first statue disappeared before she came to live with Stadler. If that's the case, it could be Katherine, Opal, or Belle."

"Or someone else who was there before Izzy and Natalie."

"Oh, and by the way," JP said, "I may have picked up another case."

Chapter 39

Wednesday morning

JP and Ron went to the sperm bank that Zack had led them to. The décor was sterile and white, probably to give the illusion that it was clean, which it appeared to be. JP asked for the manager, who came out and escorted them to his office. He had a twinkle in his eye and a slight cleft in his chin.

"I'm Vaughn Ullman. What can I do for you, gentlemen?"

"We're trying to solve a mystery involving your clinic," JP said. "How long have you worked here?"

"Thirty-three years as manager and six before that. I started this job while I was in college. When I graduated, they promoted me to manager. I've been here ever since."

"My friend here, Ron, made a donation about ten and a half years ago. He now has a woman claiming he's the father of her four-year-old child. At the time of conception, Ron was over a thousand miles away. The only way that test could've come up positive is if she used the sperm from the one-time donation he made. Can you explain how that could've happened?"

He shook his head. "No clue."

"The woman knew whose sperm she had because she named Ron as the father. How could she have accessed it by name?"

"She couldn't have. Not here. We don't offer open donor arrangements. Our service is completely anonymous. The only person who could potentially find out is a now-adult child. And that takes a court order. So, as I said, she couldn't have."

"But she did," Ron interjected.

"I really don't see how. If she came into the clinic and chose a donor, he would be anonymous. There's no way she would've been given a name."

"And yet, she got it," JP said. "Can you check the records to see if Ron's sperm was disbursed?"

"Let me see what I can do." The manager started typing on his keyboard. "Give me your full name and birthdate."

Ron gave him the information.

"Do you remember the date you came in?"

Ron gave him the year. That much he had figured out.

"Can you narrow down the date?"

"Not exactly. But I know it was in the spring, April or May, because it was close to the end of the school year."

The manager continued entering data and reading information to himself. He looked up. "Did you ever receive a check following the drop?"

"I got paid for the initial donation, but not for usage."

"So, it was never used, or you would've been paid."

"It was used once that we know of," Ron said, sounding irritated.

JP frowned at him.

"Sorry, I'm just frustrated."

The manager went back to his search. Finally, he said, "It looks like your sperm was never used." He shifted on his feet. JP wondered why he suddenly looked so nervous. "Are you sure you didn't donate somewhere else?"

Ron shook his head. "I only did it once, and it was right here."

"I don't have any answers for you."

Ron dropped his head into his hands in frustration.

"Come on," JP said. "Let's go."

Once outside, JP said, "Did you see how he shifted when he found your records? His tone even changed."

"You think he was lying?"

"Maybe. There was something fishy. I could tell by his body language."

Ron made a U-turn. "Let's go back and put some pressure on him."

"We're not thugs. And he's not going to tell us anything more, no matter what we say."

"So, that's it?"

"I'll talk to Sabre about getting a court order to see his files."

"What are the chances?"

"Probably not good, since all I have is a hunch. We'll need more, but I don't know what. Let me think about it." They were both silent for a few seconds, then JP said, "Carla had to be involved somehow. What are the chances she coincidentally got your sperm if she went to a clinic? She had to know it was yours."

"Maybe she stole it," Ron said.

"But there's still the question of how she knew it was yours. Unless she saw you go to the clinic, or followed you there."

"But we hadn't met yet."

"Maybe she had a friend working at the clinic who recognized you from somewhere and told her about your visit."

"But why?"

"I don't know."

"And why wasn't my sperm used elsewhere? I sound good on paper. There's more to this than we're seeing."

"I agree," JP said. "I just don't see how we'll figure this out. It really has me baffled. I feel like I'm pushing a rope up a hill."

When JP pulled out of the parking spot, a white SUV pulled out as well. He didn't think much about it until he made a third turn and the car was still behind him, although it had dropped back a little. He made another turn.

"Where are you going?" Ron asked.

"Just testing something."

The car behind him turned as well. JP drove three blocks and turned left.

"What the heck?" Ron asked.

"I think we're being followed."

Ron turned around. "That looks like the same car that was sitting in front of my house last night."

"What?"

"I figured it was someone visiting a neighbor."

"I'm guessing not," JP said. "See if you can get the license number."

"There's no plate on the front. Can you get him to pass you?"

"I'm not sure that's a good idea. I think I'll just lose him."

JP sped off, then made a couple of quick turns.

"He's not keeping up," Ron said.

JP drove into a parking lot and out the back side.

"I think you lost him."

"What do you think that's about?" JP asked.

"Beats me. But if it's the same car that was at my house last night, then they're probably after me, not you."

"Unless it has something to do with Stadler. You've been a presence on this case, and that was a white SUV, the same kind of vehicle Thelma saw the night of the Stadler murder."

JP drove Ron home. "You sure you don't want to hang with me today?"

"I'll be careful. No need to put you in jeopardy too, if it's me they're after."

"True. But I have a gun."

Chapter 40

Wednesday morning

JP waited in the reception area for Valerie, feeling restless. There was no one else in the sparsely decorated room. He had been there fifteen minutes, and it was already five minutes past their scheduled time. Patience wasn't his strong suit, but he waited. She was nearly fifteen minutes late when she came out to get him.

"Come on in." Valerie led him into her office, where they both sat down.

Something about her looked very familiar, but he couldn't figure out what it was. "You are Valerie Ellison, correct?"

"Yes." She didn't offer an explanation for the name change, and JP didn't think it was any of his business to ask. "Thanks for seeing me."

"Before you start asking questions, I need to reiterate that I can't tell you anything about my clients. I shouldn't even be talking to you."

"I understand. I'm a private detective for a juvenile court attorney. We're dealing with a sexual abuse case, and I believe you're somewhat of an expert. In fact, I know you have counseled at least one of his victims. The perpetrator is Ritchie Stadler."

"Perhaps I have," she said noncommittally, but her eyes showed recognition.

JP thought she'd make a lousy poker player. He also wondered how she reacted to her clients when they told her something horrible. "Someone murdered him."

She looked surprised, but quickly contained it. "That's too bad. I'm sorry for his family, if he had one. When did it happen?"

"Late last Friday night, or early Saturday morning."

"What do you need from me?"

"I was hoping you might have information that could shed some light on his murder."

"Like what?"

"Like who killed him."

"It's no secret that I'd like to rid the earth of every pedophile out there, but if you're suggesting it was me, you're way off base. I was on a red-eye flying home from a vacation in Aruba. Besides, why would I help you find someone who killed a pervert who hurts kids?"

"Because an innocent man whose child was one of Stadler's victims can't get his child back until this is resolved. That little girl deserves to be with her father."

"I'm sorry for that, but I really can't help you."

"Do you know anyone who knows him who might be capable of murder?"

"Look, Mr. Torn, even if I did, I couldn't tell you. But I don't." She got up and walked toward the door. "Your ten minutes are up, and I have another appointment. I hope you find what you're looking for."

Now that he'd ruled out Valerie and couldn't question Opal, it was time to focus on the second statue. *But was there really a second statue? If so, it wouldn't be hard to find out.* He knew just who to ask.

~~~

"Nice to see you again. Come in." Thelma opened the door for JP to pass. "Have a seat. I'll get you a Pepsi."
~~~

JP knew better than to argue with her. She would eventually just do it anyway.

"Thank you."

She returned shortly with a cold can of Pepsi.

"Perfect," he said.

"Did you find out everything you needed on that case?"

"I've learned a lot, thanks to you, but I have a few more questions."

"Go ahead."

"Do you remember a dragon statue in the front entrance of the Stadler house?"

"Yes. There were two, one on each side of the foyer. They sat on beautiful little three-legged black walnut tables with red-oak inlay. They were actually half tables, so they were flush against the wall. The red oak contrasted beautifully with the black walnut. They were eye-catching and sophisticated. In fact, the tables were gorgeous; the statues were hideous."

"How long were they there? I mean, did Ritchie acquire them or did they belong to his parents?"

"Ritchie inherited them from his paternal grandfather when he was six. It was kind of odd because I don't think Ritchie ever liked his grandfather. Nor did Ritchie's father, and he was pretty vocal about it. Maybe the old man gave them to Ritchie as a way of getting even with his son for the way he treated him, leaving his grandson the only thing of value he had."

"What were they worth?"

"The set was supposedly worth half a million back then. Who knows what the value is today?"

JP wondered if Katherine knew what her statue was worth and had disposed of it, or had plans to in the future. He hoped not. "When was the last time you saw both statues?"

She thought for a moment. "I don't remember exactly, but it was after Ritchie's mom had passed, and he was living there without her." She paused again. "But you already knew that, didn't you?"

"I had a pretty good idea. The police detective on this case says Ritchie never reported anything stolen. Do you know why?"

"No idea."

"Do you think maybe Ritchie sold it?"

"He'd never sell just one. As a pair, they were far more valuable. Besides, he loved those things for some reason. He would never have parted with either of them voluntarily."

"Do you know that the second one is gone as well?"

"Yes."

"Do you know where it went?"

"I could guess, but I won't. I was in his house and saw it was gone. I asked him about it and he said something that surprised me."

"What was that?"

"He said, 'They're ugly anyway—just like my grandfather.'"

"Do you know what he meant by that?"

"I had my own ideas about what he might have meant, but they were only conjecture. I didn't ask him. And he never did tell me what happened to the statue."

JP's phone rang. He checked and saw that it was Ron. He declined the call.

"You can get that if you need to."

"It can wait. Can you describe the statues? I have an idea, but I'm not sure how close I am."

"I can do better than that." She walked to the den and returned with a photo in a double five-by-seven frame. One picture was of her and her husband dancing. In the other, they were standing in the Stadler foyer. The statues loomed in the foreground. "There they are in all their glory."

JP studied the photo of the identical dragons sprawled across the tables, then took out his phone. "Would you mind if I took a picture?"

"Not at all. I'd give you the photo, but it's one of my favorites. I love both of those. I don't have many of us on the dance floor. Oliver could cut a rug, and when we waltzed, he made me feel like I was floating through the air."

Ron called again. "I'd better get this. It must be important."

"Go ahead."

"Hello, Ron." JP took a couple of steps away.

"I'm definitely being followed."

"Where are you?"

"I was headed to your house, but when I realized I wasn't alone, I changed my direction."

"Good. Drive toward the police station. I'll meet you there. I'll call you back as soon as I get in my truck."

JP turned back to his host.

"Is everything okay?" Thelma asked.

"I think so, but I need to go. Thanks for the photo, and I'm sorry to bother you."

"You're always welcome. Come back and see me anytime."

Chapter 41

Chapter 41

Wednesday afternoon

JP continued his conversation with Ron as he drove downtown. "Where are you?"

"About two blocks away from the station," Ron said.

"Is the car still behind you?"

"Yes."

"Is it staying close?"

"Fairly."

"Can you see who's driving?"

"All I can tell is that he's wearing a baseball cap and sunglasses. At least I think they're sunglasses."

"That's what I saw earlier," JP said. "And he's made no attempt to get closer?"

"No. I'm about to pull into the parking lot. Where are you?"

"A half mile away."

"I turned in."

"Did he follow you?"

"No. He drove on by."

"Try to see where he went, but do *not* follow him."

"Don't worry, I won't."

JP pulled into the lot just as Ron was turning around. JP pulled up alongside him. "Did you see where he went?"

"No. He disappeared into the traffic. What do we do now?" Ron asked.

"Was it the same car that followed us earlier today?"

"Yes. And I'm pretty certain it was the same one that was at my house."

JP was suddenly concerned about Sabre's mother since she lived with Ron, although she was spending more and more time at her man friend's house. "Where is your mother?" JP looked around to make sure the car had not returned.

"She's been at Harley's since Friday."

"Call her and make sure she doesn't go to the house for anything. And follow me, we're going to park."

JP found a double space, and they parked and got out.

"I called Mom." Ron scowled. "I didn't want to worry her, but I made sure she understood the gravity. She promised she wouldn't go home."

"Do you believe her?"

"She had me on speaker and Harley heard it too. He assured me he would keep her safe."

"Good." They walked toward the department, both looking around as they moved.

"Do you think this has anything to do with my stay in WITSEC?" Ron asked.

"It's not likely, but until we know who this is, we need to be careful."

Ron shook his head. "I thought that was all over."

"Hopefully, it is. But for now, we'll report it to Wells, in case it's connected to Stadler. Then you need to call the feds. Do you still have your contact?"

"Yes. I'll call him."

"We need to find another place for you to stay. I'd take you to our place, but I don't want to put Sabre or the kids at risk."

"I don't either," Ron said. "Hey, maybe I could stay at Sabre's condo."

"We'll make that decision after you talk to your WITSEC contact. For now, let's go see if Wells is here."

On the way into the building, JP called Sabre and explained the situation. As far as he knew, there was no reason to believe anyone was in danger except possibly Ron.

"Will you call Conner? I'm not sure I'll be home before he gets there, but I'll make sure I'm there before the girls get home. I'll pick them up myself. Where will you be?"

"I'm at court for the duration of the day. And yes, I'll let the marshals know, so don't worry about me."

"Okay. Please call me before you leave court." JP hung up.

They found Detective Wells in his cubicle eating lunch. When they explained the situation, Wells made note of where Ron would be staying and said he would get a patrol car to pass by occasionally.

As they walked out, Ron called his contact at WITSEC and told him.

"What did he say?" JP asked.

"He thinks it's unlikely, but he will do some checking and get back to me."

"Considering the type of vehicle, it's more likely something to do with the Stadler murder. Remember? Thelma saw a white SUV in the neighborhood around the time Stadler was killed. Maybe you got closer than we know."

"All I did was find Melodi."

"It could be her husband. He's a bit of a wildcard." JP paused. "But Wells said he was on a fishing trip in Mexico when Stadler was killed. Wells checked out the alibi himself. And Akroyd drives an old pickup."

"Melodi was driving an old gray Nissan. The only other connection I found was Belle. I can't imagine why she would follow me. Oh, and by the way, I followed up on Natalie's alibi, and it checked out. Both women vouched for her and employees at two of the bars also remembered seeing her. She's in the clear."

"That's good to know," JP said. "For now, we either need to get you some place where you can hole up, which would be my choice, or get you a different vehicle. I'd swap with you, but he obviously knows my truck, so that won't work."

"I just don't want to put anyone else in danger. If the guy is a thug from my old mistake, then this should only be on me."

"I won't hang you out to dry. Sabre would never forgive me. Besides, you're the closest thing I have to a brother."

"What do you mean? You have two brothers—Troy and Gene."

"I never see Troy, and Gene is in prison. So, you're all I've got right now." JP smiled. "Here's what we're going to do. We'll leave your car here for now, and you're coming with me. You can keep a lookout in case we pick up a tail."

"Where are we going?"

"Does it matter?"

"Not really."

Chapter 42

Chapter 42

Wednesday afternoon

JP drove slowly out of the police headquarters parking lot, hoping he would pick up the tail. He zigzagged through the downtown streets to see if someone followed, but no one did. Neither spoke as they looked around for the white SUV.

The silence was broken when Ron's phone rang. "It's my contact from WITSEC." He answered and put the call on speaker. "What did you find out?" Ron asked.

"I can't find anything that would point to the men you were dealing with. Their operation was totally dismantled, and all the leaders are dead. An adult daughter who went into the program is still there. She likes her new life and doesn't want to change it."

"So, you think it's unlikely any of them are involved?"

"Quite sure. We wouldn't have let you out of the program if we thought it wasn't safe. It's rare that we do, but your case warranted it."

"Thanks," Ron said.

"I don't know what you've got yourself into, Brown, but you need to look closer to home."

"I've been doing some investigating for a PI firm, it's probably something to do with that."

"Good luck."

Ron hung up. "That's a relief. I think."

"Most definitely. We can handle the local yokels. The mob is another story. What do you want to do?"

"I need to get some grub, then I think I'll stay at Sabre's condo tonight. I'll decide in the morning what to do next."

JP drove him back to his car. "Where are you stopping for food?"

"I was thinking I'd go to Maritza's. That was so good."

"I'll follow you, but I'll drop back a little to make sure no one is on your tail. I'll stay with you to the restaurant and then to the condo. Maybe we can catch this guy, or at least get a license plate number."

Everything went as planned, without sighting the white SUV. After Ron went into the condo, JP hung out in his truck to make sure no one showed up. He gave it half an hour, then left, certain they hadn't been followed.

As he drove away, he called Wells to see if he had an update.

"We know it's not Uri Moss," Detective Wells said.

"How?"

"He's been in a hospital in Colorado since Thursday. He went there to see a friend, then hit a deer, crashed his car, and was unconscious for several days."

"I was hoping he was our guy."

"Not him. I've also checked out other people who were bilked by Stadler, and so far, nothing. A lot of anger, but no potential killers. Besides, the murder seems too personal."

"Any luck on the murder weapon?"

"We have someone looking through photos of the train room, but so far we can't determine if anything is missing. According to Heidi, Stadler never got rid of any pieces he had acquired, so it's fairly easy to track the old stuff, but time consuming. He has flash drives with train pics, and we're sorting through those for anything he might have bought in the last few years to see if any are missing. It's a daunting task, and I'm not sure how much good it will do if we find that a piece is gone."

"If we know what we're looking for, that could help us find it, maybe even lead us to the killer."

"Do you have anything else for me?" Wells asked. "Because we like Grady Harn more and more for this homicide. He has the same kind of vehicle Thelma saw the night of the murder. He has no alibi. He attacked Stadler in open court, so imagine what he might do in private. And Dakota's reaction to the model trains adds another layer."

"What does that have to do with it?"

"I think Dakota told her father about the train room. There's a reason that room was destroyed and nothing else in the house."

"Then all Stadler's victims and their loved ones are suspects."

"That's true. So, what can you tell me about his victims? I think you know more than you're sharing. We're at a complete loss there. No one wants to talk about it." The detective sounded frustrated. "We did get some information from Evan Green, the deputy sheriff who lives a few doors down from Stadler. He told us he talked to you, so I imagine you got the same thing we did. We haven't been able to track anyone because he didn't know the women's surnames."

"Yes. He told me what he knew."

"He sent us to Thelma, but she couldn't seem to remember much either. So, what do you know that we don't?"

"I've been hitting a lot of dead ends too." JP told him about Izzy Hernandez and her daughter Natalie, hoping it would prompt the department to investigate Izzy's death—and possibly move their suspicion away from Harn. "We checked out Natalie's alibi and it seems valid, so I don't think she's our perp, but I'm sure you'll determine that yourself, maybe even find something I didn't."

Chapter 43

Chapter 43

Wednesday evening

Ron sat at the kitchen counter in Sabre's condo and ate the tacos he'd picked up at Maritza's. He took a bottle of beer from the refrigerator and sat down on the sofa in the front room. He clicked on the TV and finally relaxed for the first time that day. Seconds later, the doorbell rang. Ron hurried to the window and pulled back the shade just enough to see out. He couldn't believe it—a white SUV was parked out front. *How had they found him?* The doorbell rang again. Ron couldn't see who it was from the window, so he peeked through the peephole. Standing there ringing the doorbell was Carla. *Was she alone? Or was someone else in the SUV?*

He didn't answer the door. Instead, he went back to the window to see if anyone else got out of the SUV. He saw no movement and the car appeared to be empty. He sent a text to JP.

Ron: *Carla is at my door. A white SUV parked in front of condo. Don't know if they're related.*

JP: *Stall. I'm about five minutes away.*

The doorbell continued to ring.

"Answer the door," Carla yelled. "I know you're in there."

Ron didn't want to deal with Carla alone, and he still didn't know if that was her car or someone else's. He kept silent, but she started banging on the door and yelling, getting louder and louder with every demand. Soon neighbors started shouting at Carla, and she bellowed back. Ron finally decided he'd better let her in and calm her down. He wasn't physically afraid of her, but he didn't feel equipped to deal with her emotionally.

Ron moved back and forth between the window and the peephole in the door, watching for a second person or some movement in the SUV. He saw no one but Carla, but he didn't have a good vantage point. He ran upstairs and looked out the window. He could see Carla at the door, but he couldn't see anyone else. Carla kept yelling, and a neighbor threatened to call the police. Ron hurried back down, opened the door, and glanced around. She was the only one in sight.

"Get in here." Ron let her pass by, then closed the door quickly and locked it. "Carla! What the heck are you doing?"

"I just came to see you, darling."

"What are you driving?"

"That's a strange question."

"Just tell me."

"A white Hyundai SUV. Why?"

"Have you been following me around town?"

She shrugged. "Yes."

"Why?"

"That's a silly question."

"Why have you been following me?"

"Because you won't come home. My husband should be home. We should be together as a family."

"Carla, I don't live with you, and I'm not your husband."

Just then Ron's phone beeped with a text. He reached for his phone in his pocket, but before he could get it, Carla threw her arms around him, holding tight.

"Yes, you are!"

Ron grabbed her arms and pulled her off him. "I am not," he said forcefully. "You need to think. I am not your husband."

"Why do you keep saying that?"

"Because it's the truth."

"Did you divorce me?" Carla threw her arms in the air and yelled, "Why would you do that?"

"We were never married."

The doorbell rang. "Ron!" JP called out. "Open up."

Ron opened the door and let JP in.

Carla kept talking. "But God wanted it that way. God brought us a beautiful little girl for us to raise."

"Hi, Carla," JP said.

"Will you please remind Ron that we're married. I'm sure Bob told you about the ceremony, but Ron can't remember." She turned to Ron. "How could you not remember? That doesn't make any sense."

JP put his hand gently on her shoulder. "Carla, why don't we sit down and talk about it?" He led her to the sofa, but she reached back and grabbed Ron's hand.

"You come too."

Ron sat down next to her, but pulled his hand free. He wished he knew how to handle the situation, but he wouldn't give her any encouragement. Then he wondered if he should just humor her.

JP got her to make eye contact with him. "Carla, is that your white SUV?"

"Yes. Why is everyone so worried about my car?"

"We're not. Sorry. Have you been following Ron for the last two days?"

"Yes."

"Were you wearing a baseball cap and sunglasses?"

"Yes."

"We're concerned because we didn't know who it was. We were afraid Ron was in danger. Can you understand that?"

She lowered her gaze and said softly, "I guess I shouldn't have done that, but he didn't come home." Her voice started to rise again.

"It's all right now, Carla," JP said. "Everything's going to be okay. You just sit here and talk to Ron for a few minutes."

JP got up and went into the kitchen. Ron tried to keep Carla calm while he was gone, but she seemed so agitated. He wondered how he could ever handle this if he accepted paternity or if the court found him legally responsible.

JP returned shortly and sat back down. He tried to engage Carla, but she couldn't keep her attention directed anywhere but on Ron. They both asked questions about Liberty once they discovered that was her favorite subject. Carla really seemed to love the little girl, but it was almost as if she was her friend instead of her mother.

It wasn't long before the doorbell rang.

JP jumped up from the sofa. "I'll get it." He walked to the door and let Carla's sister in.

"Hi, Emma," Carla said. "What are you doing here? I mean, it's nice of you to come see us, but I didn't expect you." She turned to Ron. "Did you know she was coming, honey?"

"I'm glad she's here." He sighed and looked at Emma. "Thanks for coming."

"No problem." She sat next to Carla where JP had been sitting. "Liberty is missing you. You need to come home with me and see her."

Carla turned to Ron. "Do you mind if I go? I'm sorry, but Liberty needs me."

"You need to go to her then."

They all stood, and Carla kissed Ron quickly on the lips.

After they left, Ron collapsed into the sofa. "I'm not sure I can do this. It's exhausting."

"But at least we know it wasn't the mob after you."

"That might be easier to handle."

Chapter 44

Thursday morning

Ron walked along the beach, trying to clear his head. In a few days, he would be starting his new job as CEO of Silent Thunder Charity. He wanted to be excited about it, but he just had too much else eating at him. Before he would be fit to do anything, he had to make a decision about his *daughter*. He tried taking Carla and himself out of the equation and just thinking about what was best for Liberty. But no matter how he played out the scenario, he couldn't detach from it. He needed someone to bounce this off of. He immediately thought of Lana and called her.

"Are you busy?"

"Not really," Lana said.

"I'd like to run a couple things past you. Do you mind?"

"About the paternity issue?"

"Yes."

"Did you find the lab?"

"I did, and I'll text you that information. But right now, I'm wrestling with what to do about the whole thing." Ron would much rather have had this conversation in person so he could see her reaction. He hoped he wasn't overstepping.

"I'm not sure I'm the right person to discuss this with," Lana said. "I've never had a child. In fact, I've never spent much time around children. I'm not sure I was ever a kid myself."

She laughed softly. "But this isn't about me. What are your thoughts?"

"I'm sure I could be a good father, but Liberty already has Roger. Does she need another father? And if he continues to raise her, Carla will forever be in his life. After what happened last night, I'm not sure I could handle it."

"What happened?"

Ron told her about being followed and Carla showing up at Sabre's condo. "That kind of scene couldn't be good for the little girl. My presence obviously makes Carla spiral out of control, and that will affect Liberty. According to Sabre and Liberty's attorney, she's a happy little girl who has learned to cope with her unconventional mother."

"You still haven't seen the child?"

"No. I keep wondering if I should. Maybe that would help me decide what to do. But I'm afraid to do that. What if I fall in love with her instantly? I love children and always thought I'd be a father someday—but not like this. Maybe I should just leave it up to fate. If the court determines I'm the father, legal or otherwise, then maybe I should step up, and if it doesn't, then walk away. But that doesn't seem right either. Nothing about this seems right. What do you think?"

"You're right. Nothing about this is right or fair. But life is like that. We play the hand we're dealt."

"That's it? No words of advice?"

"I told you, I'm not really the one to advise you. I'm not in your shoes." Lana took a deep breath. "I'll tell you this much. I don't think you should see her until you decide. There's no reason to confuse her, and you'll probably fall in love with her because she's a kid and you love kids, yours or not. I hear you talk about Conner and Morgan. You're crazy about those kids, and you're not related to them. Blood or DNA isn't the issue here. That is only going to matter as far as legal responsibility."

"Sabre says that if I go forward with the paternity trial and the judge rules I'm not the legal father, then my paternal rights do not exist and I have no choice. If I try to see her, I'm just a stalker."

"So, that's the only decision you need to make right now. Whether to go forward with the trial, knowing it could take away any possibility of parenting that child."

"Which brings me back to what's best for Liberty."

"Exactly."

"You've been absolutely no help," Ron said with a teasing tone.

"I told you I wasn't the one to ask. But if you want tech help, let me know. I may be able to figure out what happened to your sperm sample."

Ron saw a man headed toward the ocean carrying a surfboard. "I think that's Zack. Do you mind if I call you back in a bit?"

Ron walked in his direction, closing the gap.

"Zack?" he called out when he got closer.

"Wow. That's twice this week. Were you looking for me again?"

"No. I was just out walking, clearing my head."

"You should go surfing. That'll do it every time."

"Maybe I will."

"Did you find the clinic you were looking for?" Zack sounded clear headed. Maybe he didn't indulge when he surfed.

"I found it and thanks for that. They weren't much help though. They just told me the sample wasn't ever used and they can't explain what happened."

"Why don't you ask to withdraw it? Buy it back. If it hasn't been used, they have to give it to you."

"I didn't know that."

"At least that's the way it used to work. The laws could've changed, I guess."

"Thanks. I'll have my lawyer check into it."

"No problem. Speaking of the clinic, whatever happened to that knockout girl you were dating from there?"

"What are you talking about?"

"You started dating her right around the end of the school year. She would come to the coffee shop we hung out at. She had dark hair and was drop-dead gorgeous."

"You must mean Carla."

"Maybe. I was never good with names."

"What does she have to do with the clinic?"

"She worked there."

"What?" Ron's mouth dropped open.

"You didn't know that?"

"No. Are you sure?"

"Yeah. I saw her at the clinic many times, including the day we all went together. You guys were so nervous, you didn't notice much of anything. I tried to get her to go out with me, but she never would. Then you got her attention in the coffee shop, and I gave up. I never saw either of you much after that."

Chapter 45

Chapter 45

Thursday morning

Sabre moseyed out of the bedroom and into the kitchen. JP was sitting at the kitchen table with a cup of coffee and a bowl of Cheerios.

"Happy Thanksgiving," Sabre mumbled.

"You too, sweetheart." He nodded toward the teapot. "I've got your water boiling."

"Thank you." Sabre dropped a piece of bread in the toaster, then made her tea. Just as she set her cup on the table next to JP, her toast popped up. She spread chunky peanut butter and apricot jam on it and sat down. "How's the Stadler investigation going?"

"I'm having more fun than a mosquito in a blood bank."

"Then why do you look so stressed?"

"I've never had so many suspects and no hard evidence for any of them." JP gestured with his thumb and index finger. "I'm this close to taking it all to Detective Wells and dumping it on him."

"Why don't you?"

"Because it probably won't help our client, and it could potentially get some really nice person in serious trouble."

"You still think it might be Katherine, don't you?"

"She's our most likely suspect, and I'd hate to see her go to jail for killing that slime ball." He shook his head. "Even worse, what if it leads to Opal? I'd hate to see anyone do time for ridding the earth of one more pervert. How wrong can that be?"

"You don't really believe that."

"I don't?"

Sabre ignored him. "So, what now?"

"I'll visit Grady again and do a little more research on Heidi since you told me about the change in Stadler's trust. It gives her a stronger motive, especially if she knew about the change."

"She's already admitted to that. Do you think that'll be enough to divert Wells' attention away from Grady?"

"Except that his daughter benefits from Stadler's death, so it might be just more circumstantial evidence against our client. Wells may even think Grady and Heidi were in it together."

"So, the question is still: What now?"

"I'll keep my saddle oiled and gun greased."

"And you'll figure it out."

"That's what I said."

~~~

JP called Grady, who agreed to meet with him. When he arrived, Grady was waiting for him in his garage.

"I hope you don't mind meeting out here."

"This is fine," JP said. "I apologize for taking up your holiday. I just have a few questions."

"No problem. I didn't have anything going on this morning anyway. Dakota is allowed to spend the day with me at my brother's house. My brother can't pick her up until noon. So, this is fine."

"Grady, do you think Heidi could've murdered Stadler?"

His eyebrows shot up in surprise. "She's not a violent person. And didn't you say his murder was premeditated?"

"It looks that way."
~~~

"I don't believe she could do that. She doesn't think he did anything to Dakota, so why would she want to kill him?"

JP furrowed his brow in disbelief. "How could she not believe her daughter?"

"She accepts that Dakota was molested, but she thinks it had to be someone else. Maybe someone she's afraid to tell on."

"What do you think?"

"There's no doubt in my mind that Stadler did it. I think Heidi is blinded by the glitz and glamour of her life with him."

"She'll have it all now."

Grady tilted his head in a questioning gesture. "What do you mean?"

"We just found out that Stadler recently changed his trust and left everything to Farrah and Dakota with Heidi as their trustee."

"You're suggesting she had a motive to kill him?"

"It looks like it."

Grady shook his head. "I can't believe Heidi would commit murder. At least not premeditated."

"Maybe she came home unexpectedly, witnessed something, and just lost it."

"It would've had to have been something awful. Even so, I can't see Heidi getting angry enough to kill someone. She's selfish, and a little bossy, but she's not a mean or violent person."

"I want you to know that the new trust could throw more suspicion on you simply because it benefits your daughter," JP said.

"That's not good, but I'm glad Dakota will get something out of this."

"We're doing everything we can to find who really killed Stadler."

"I appreciate that. Most of the time I'm not too worried because I know I didn't do it, so they won't find any evidence that I did. I just don't like that it has slowed down my reunification with my little girl."

Chapter 46

Chapter 46

Thursday afternoon

Sabre and her family entered Harley's house, with Sabre carrying a bottle of wine. She had offered to bring a dish, but her mother wouldn't hear of it. Her mother loved to cook and to entertain. She was a perfect match for Harley.

Beverly hugged each of the kids and said in a hushed voice, "There's presents for all of you in the living room."

"Mom, you don't need to do that every time you see the kids."

"I don't do it every time, just when I feel like it. And I feel like it a lot."

"Thanks, Grandma," Morgan said as she and the others darted off.

Beverly beamed. "That makes it all worth it. I don't know if you or Ron will ever have any children, and you know how much I want to be a grandma. So, let me have this." Just then Ron walked in the door. "And there he is, my other childless child."

Ron's face lost color. He glanced at Sabre with a questioning look. She shook her head, ever so slightly.

"Mom was just complaining about us not making her a grandmother."

Ron took a breath, hugged his mother, and said, "Maybe someday, Mom, when I grow up."

It wasn't long before Travis arrived. Sabre escorted him to the backyard where the men were sitting around chatting. "I'll let Dené know you're here."

Sabre found the girl in the den playing video games with Conner. "Travis is here."

Dené looked up and smiled, a big improvement from a few weeks ago. "Pause it, Conner," Dené said. "I'll be right back." She jumped up.

"One game, then you kids come outside and get some sunshine."

"I'm going out now," Morgan said, following Dené out the door.

Sabre watched out the glass door as Dené approached her father. She had a quick encounter, then ran back inside to her game. Sabre went to the kitchen to help her mother.

"How are Dené and Travis getting along?"

"They're making progress. She actually seems happy to see him. I don't think she's ready to live with him yet, but they are definitely moving in the right direction. Thanks for inviting him here today."

"Of course. He's family too. And I couldn't leave him to those crazy siblings of his."

Sabre laughed. "I'm sure he'd go it alone before spending the day with them."

Harley made regular trips from the kitchen to the backyard with plates of *hors d'oeuvres*. The drinks were readily available in the refrigerator on the patio.

"Mom, they'll be too full to eat dinner if you keep sending out appetizers."

"No one is ever too full for Thanksgiving dinner. Besides, we have a couple of hours before we sit."

Harley came back inside with an empty plate. "Sabre, they want you for a fourth in cornhole. Travis and Ron have challenged you and JP."

"I need to help ..."

"Go on. I'll help your mother. We've become quite a team in the kitchen."

"You heard him, Sabey. I'm almost done here for a while. I'll join you in a bit."

Sabre smiled and kissed her mother on the cheek, thinking her mom would never stop calling her by her childhood nickname.

The sun was shining and the temperature was about seventy-two degrees, a perfect day to be outside. Sabre joined the others in cornhole, which got competitive. Harley and Beverly came out, and Harley played a game of horseshoes with Morgan. It wasn't long before Conner and Dené joined them, and Morgan and Dené played against Harley and Conner. The girls won two out of three games, but Sabre was sure the guys had gone easy on them.

They sat down to dinner at four o'clock at a beautifully decorated table that looked like something in a magazine photo. Sabre knew her mother was in her element. She had always made holidays special for them growing up, but now she had the means to do it right. Sabre missed her father, but she was happy her mother had found someone else to love.

Beverly had the girls help her serve dessert, and Harley brought the coffee pot around for those who wanted it. Sabre had just taken her first bite of pumpkin pie when she felt her phone vibrate. She glanced at it and saw it was from Bob. She didn't answer. He was probably just calling to wish her a happy Thanksgiving.

A few seconds later, Ron's phone rang. He pulled it out of his pocket and shut off the sound. "Sorry, I forgot to turn off the volume." Sabre and Ron both knew how much their mother disapproved of phone calls at the dinner table.

Ron was sitting directly across the table from Sabre and she caught his eye, then mouthed, *Bob?*

He nodded.

Sabre looked over in time to see JP's phone light up and whispered. "See if it's Bob."

He checked his phone under the table and turned it so Sabre could see that Bob had called him too. Now she was concerned. Before she could excuse herself from the table, her mother said, "Sabre Brown, go check your phone message. You're obviously worried about something."

Sabre stood. "Thanks, Mom." She left the room and listened to her message as she walked to the patio. Bob had simply said, "Call me. It's urgent." When she did, Bob picked up immediately. "Carla is back in the hospital."

"What happened?"

"She tried to kill herself again."

"That's terrible."

"Emma said Carla tried to overdose."

"On cough syrup again?"

"No. She had just filled a prescription for Klonopin and took half the pills at once."

"Do you know what set her off?" Sabre asked.

"She wrote a note." Bob stopped, apparently hesitant to tell.

"What is it?"

"She said she couldn't take it anymore. That Ron didn't love her and didn't want to be her husband. She said he asked for a divorce."

"Poor woman."

"Last night, Carla stayed with Roger and Emma, who kept checking on her. Carla made it through the night, but then today she hardly got out of bed. Emma went to see how she was and caught Carla taking the pills and called right away for an ambulance."

"How is Carla physically?"

"She's going to be okay, but she'll be committed for a while. That's two attempts within a month."

"Thanks, Bob, for letting me know. I'm with Ron, so I'll tell him."

Sabre returned to the dining room. "Ron, I need to talk to you."

He followed her back to the patio. "What's wrong?"

"Carla is back in the hospital. She tried to commit suicide again."

Chapter 47

Friday morning

Ron had a restless night's sleep. He wondered if he should attempt to see Carla. He wanted to help her, but he was afraid his presence would do more harm than good. He struggled with the choice he had to make about Liberty. He awoke feeling he had reached an epiphany. He got up, brushed his teeth, and called Lana.

"I've made a decision." He first told her about Carla's suicide attempt, then added, "I need to get out of Carla's life and stay out of it. It's not good for her, and that can't be good for Liberty."

"What can I do to help?"

"I need you to check the records at the sperm bank. I just found out that Carla was an employee during the time I donated. She must've stolen my sperm and kept it somewhere until she decided to use it. If you could find out how that was done so I can confront the manager, perhaps we can get a confirmation that will get me declared not legally responsible for Liberty. If I stay away from Carla, it just might save her life."

"I'll call you when I have something."

Ron felt like a weight had lifted from his shoulders. Deciding was always the hardest part. Now, he could make a plan. He called Sabre and told her his thinking. "Lana will see what she can find out about Carla's employment at the clinic and about my donation."

"You realize we won't be able to use any of that in court, right?"

"But we'll know what questions to ask, and the clinic could be in for a huge lawsuit if they don't cooperate."

"That's true, Bro."

"Have you heard anything more about Carla?"

"She's doing well, considering. She'll move to another facility today or tomorrow and be on a seventy-two-hour hold. My guess is they'll have a hearing, find that she's a danger to herself, and keep her there a lot longer. These two attempts were far too close to completion to risk letting her out on her own any time soon."

~~~

Lana got on her laptop in Clarice's trailer and started the research for Ron. She had the name of the fertility clinic, so she just had to find a way inside. That was the easy part. Within twenty minutes, she was checking records. The time-consuming part would be reading through all the information. She started with employee records to see if Carla had actually worked there. Having an approximate timeframe narrowed her search. And there it was.

Carla Noel Larkin, employee number 47471, began her employment on January fourth and left on the twentieth of May, just a little over four months. Ron had told her he met Carla at the coffee shop on May nineteenth. He knew the date because Carla had insisted they celebrate it as their anniversary. Carla had quit the day after, and her employment record was flagged with *DO NOT REHIRE.*

It took a great deal more research and perusing to find that the comment was connected to sperm donor #33323. The donor records had more security built around them than the website itself, but within an hour Lana found that #33323 was none other than Ronald Adrian Brown.
~~~

Lana called Ron to give him the information. "Carla didn't handle your collection, which is probably why you didn't recognize her when you saw her in the coffee shop. After the collector logged it, the container went to another employee who checked it to make sure it matched the donor and catalogued it. Carla handled it from there. She mixed it with the cryo-preservative solution, divided it into aliquots, sealed it into vials, and put it in the nitrogen storage unit."

"What happened to it after that?"

"No one knows. Your number and generic information are still listed, but it appears that your sperm was gone not long after it was deposited."

"How can you tell?"

"There was a request for your sperm about a week later, but it was denied. There are some cryptic notes in the file that indicate they couldn't find it. After that, your file is tagged and no longer listed as available. Some kind of investigation followed, but the notes are vague."

"They just covered it up and figured no one would ever know."

"That's my guess."

"So, Carla must've seen me and chose me to be the future father of her child."

"Then she either made a point to meet you, or she 'accidentally' ran into you at the coffee shop. Maybe she thought she could have her family the old-fashioned way when you started dating her, so she kept it stored somewhere until five years ago and then got pregnant."

"Wouldn't there be a record at a hospital or clinic somewhere when she got impregnated?"

"Not necessarily. These things can be done at home. It may have taken several tries, but she took all the vials so she had enough sperm for more than one attempt. There are kits that can be used at home, as long as the donation has been cryopreserved. She may even still have some. Who knows?"

"What do you mean *all* the vials? I only went once."

"They got nine vials from that one ejaculation."

"Nine? That seems like a lot."

"It could be anywhere between one and ten vials. The average is about four or five. So, yeah, it was a lot."

Chapter 48

Friday early afternoon

Sabre read through the notes Ron had given her while she waited for Emma to arrive. She had considered having the conversation with Emma on the phone, but decided the exchange needed to be in person. Emma had agreed to meet Sabre at her office on her lunch break. She really wanted to see Liberty, but she agreed with Ron that it was better for them to stay away while things were in limbo. Emma appeared to be on board with that.

She seemed a little nervous when she arrived, but Sabre put her at ease. "Thanks for coming here."

"I appreciate that you want what's best for Liberty, just as we do."

"We all do, especially Ron," Sabre said. "How's Carla doing?"

"Better. I'm just so worried that one of these days, she'll succeed at one of her attempts. I love my sister and don't want anything to happen to her. And Liberty loves her too, although most of the time, they are more like sisters than mother and daughter."

"I know it's challenging. I've dealt with my share of mental illness, and I know it's not Carla's fault she's sick."

"Most of the time I remember that too."

"When did Carla first tell you Ron was the father of her child?"

"When she was a few months pregnant."

"Did she tell you she was dating him again?"

"She was evasive about the whole thing. I encouraged her to contact him and let him know, but she refused. She kept saying she couldn't. That he wouldn't understand. She had a rough time through her pregnancy, both physically and mentally. She had me very worried."

"I recently discovered that Carla worked at a sperm bank some years ago. Did you know that?"

"Yes. It wasn't very long though, only a few months."

"You know that Ron was in the Witness Protection Program when Carla conceived, right?"

"That's what I've been told." Emma paused. "You think Carla got Ron's sperm from the sperm bank?"

"Yes. Do you know anything about that?"

Emma was silent for few seconds, but from her facial expression Sabre was certain she knew more. Sabre waited for Emma to speak.

"I don't know anything for sure, but I'm afraid that all makes sense. Carla is a smart woman. She was a science major in college and knows her way around a lab. That's how she got that job. It was easy to find clerical workers, but she was qualified to work in the lab. That's why I was surprised when she quit."

"Did she give you any reason for leaving the lab?"

"No."

"She left the day after Ron made his deposit. And soon after, they discovered his vials were missing."

"My sister is not a thief, but she probably believed the sperm belonged to her. When she fixates on something, she becomes very possessive, and she has always been that way toward Ron. It's all part of her illness. She was so happy when she was dating him. We had high hopes for her."

"I always loved Carla. For a long time, I expected her to become a part of our family. I hate that she is suffering so."

"We all do."

"Looking back, were there any other red flags from Carla that made you suspicious about her pregnancy?"

Emma took a deep breath. "She told me it took four tries and several months to get pregnant, but it finally worked. At the time, I thought she was trying to have a baby. You know, the old-fashioned way. I never thought it was Ron, because I knew they had broken up. But now that I know Ron was out of state all that time, it doesn't make much sense. I know Carla didn't leave southern California and the best I could tell she didn't have a boyfriend. When she told me it was Ron's baby, I figured he must have been back in town."

Four tries. That meant there could still be five vials left. "Do you know if there are any vials left?"

"I didn't know any existed in the first place."

"Now that you know, do you have any idea where she might've stored them?"

"No. Sorry."

Chapter 49

Friday afternoon

JP and Sabre entered the sperm bank and asked for Vaughn Ullman. This time they were armed with more information, and a subpoena for the manager to testify.

"What can I do for you today?"

"I was in here a few days ago with Ron Brown and you checked on his donation to this facility about fifteen years ago."

"I remember you."

"I'm Ron's attorney, Sabre Brown. I'm also his sister, so I have a personal interest in this matter. If you recall, a woman is claiming that Ron is the father of her child. He hasn't seen the woman in eight years, and the child is four. The only explanation is that she took the sperm donation Ron made and had herself impregnated."

"As I explained the other day, that is not possible. Our security is very tight and it just couldn't happen."

Sabre didn't acknowledge his words. "The mother of this child is a woman named Carla Larkin. She was an employee at the time of Ron's deposit."

The manager shifted in his seat. Sabre figured he was surprised they knew that much. "My client is in a very precarious situation. All he wants is to prove that he has no legal responsibility to this child. To do that, we will need information from you, or we will get court orders to get that information."

"That's what you'll need to do."

"Here's the problem for you. In juvenile court where this issue is being contested, it will be difficult to get a subpoena duces tecum for those records. However, if we file a lawsuit against your company, we will surely get every record we need. I don't offer that as a threat. I merely want you to understand that all we're looking for is the paternity issue to be resolved. We do not want to sue, but we will if we have to."

The manager took a deep breath. Sabre got the impression he wanted to help, but felt like he couldn't.

"We already know Carla worked here. You can verify those dates for us to take into court."

"Not without permission from the employee."

"I understand that. Just so you know, we already know that Carla quit the day after Ron donated his sperm. And that there was some issue with her confiscating Ron's sperm. We know that Ron's sperm was not available for sale after only one week from the time of his donation. We know that you are the one who discovered the missing sperm, and you are the one who accepted Carla's resignation. I think you stumbled across the problem and nipped it in the bud by getting rid of the culprit. And then marked her file so she wouldn't be re-hired."

"How would you know that?"

Sabre didn't respond, she just continued. "What you didn't do is follow up and inform the donor or try to make amends. I'm guessing you didn't do that because under normal circumstances, no one would've ever known the sperm was missing."

"How are you getting all this information?" Vaughn asked.

"What matters is that we have it. Now, we can take this to the company's legal team, and file a lawsuit for damages. We both know that will take a long time and a lot of resources, not to mention that a child will be in limbo. I don't want that, and I'm guessing you don't either. So, what do you say?"

The manager rubbed his chin nervously. "I'll work with you. What do you need?"

"I need to know what happened here."

"You already know everything I know."

"So, tell me and I'll record it."

"I don't know about that." He squirmed uncomfortably.

"Then tell me, and JP will take notes and write it in his report. We should be able to get that into evidence and avoid calling you into court."

"And if you can't?"

"Then you'll be called to testify." Sabre knew he was getting more uncomfortable with the whole thing, so she added, "Look, you can do all this without involving corporate in the mess. Your job shouldn't be affected at all. Anything that happens in juvenile court is confidential. That's not true with other lawsuits."

He took a deep breath and spilled. "Carla worked here for about four months." He checked the computer and gave the exact dates. "I discovered some vials were missing when someone chose #33323 as their donor. I couldn't be sure what happened, but the other people who had handled the vials were trusted employees. They had both been with me for over two years with no issues. So, the likely culprit was Carla." His eyes clouded with pain.

"Things were shaky for me at the time. My wife had cancer, and I wasn't at the top of my game. Several errors were made in the lab, all my fault, and corporate was not happy with me. A mistake of that magnitude would have cost me my job if I'd come clean. Besides, there was little or no chance anyone would ever find out. I certainly never factored in this scenario. I meant to go through a process of paperwork that showed the sperm was contaminated, because that would have taken it off the shelf and covered my butt. But I had so much on my plate, I never did that." He paused. "I really feel terrible about what this situation has caused. I never imagined anything like this would happen, but I know that's why we have to be so careful."

"I appreciate that," Sabre said. "By the way, how's your wife?" She was reluctant to ask, but it felt appropriate.

"She hung on for six agonizing months. But she was in so much pain, it was a relief when it was finally over."

"I'm so sorry to hear that." Sabre's phone buzzed, and Grady Harn popped up on her caller ID. She ignored it.

"It was long ago. My family is doing okay now. Anyway, that's all I know. Are we good?"

"I'll need you to testify at the paternity trial, if it comes to that. I'm hoping the issue can be resolved without you, but if it can't, then you will be called." Sabre nodded at JP, who handed him the subpoena. Sabre stood. "We'll do everything we can to settle this without your testimony, but please make yourself available for that date, just in case." Sabre's phone buzzed again. This time with a text message. She glanced at the caller. It was Grady again. The message read:

Urgent. Please call.

"Thank you, sir. We'll be in touch."

Sabre called Grady as they left the room. "What's up, Grady?"

"The cops are here with a search warrant."

"We'll be right there."

~~~

Police officers had already started the search before Sabre and JP arrived. Grady met them outside.

"Let me see the warrant."

The search area included the house, the garage, any out buildings, and their motor vehicles. They were looking for the murder weapon, most likely a model train. "Where's Wells?"

"He's inside."
~~~

Sabre and JP stepped up to the door with Grady close behind. An officer stopped them from going in. JP explained who they were and said, "We need to talk to Detective Wells."

The cop turned and yelled into the house, "Hey, Wells, Harn's attorney is here to see you."

The detective came from the hall. "I can't say this is a surprise."

"It is to us," Sabre snapped. "What's going on?"

"There appears to be a missing train car. We have reason to believe it's the murder weapon."

"But you have no reason to believe the train car is in this house." Sabre waved the warrant in the air. "How did you get a judge to sign this with such flimsy evidence? This is ludicrous."

"The judge didn't think so."

Just then an officer came into the living room carrying a boxed train set. "And there you go," Wells said.

"That's the train I put under the tree at Christmas every year," Grady said.

"Should I take it?" the officer asked.

"Bag it and keep looking."

"That's ridiculous," Sabre said. "You're looking for an individual car that came from Stadler's, not the man's Christmas decorations."

"Let 'em have it," Grady said. "I'm sure Dakota will never want that under the tree again."

Chapter 50

Chapter 50

Saturday morning

"Ah, the sound of silence." Sabre walked into the den where JP sat at his desk. She came up behind him and started rubbing his shoulders.

"That feels great," JP said. "I know Travis picked up Dené and Morgan, but where is Conner this morning?"

"He went for a hike with Aiden."

"What's on your agenda today?"

"I've got prep work to do for my hearings Monday morning, and in the afternoon, I have Ron's paternity case. I want to make sure I'm ready for that."

"You expect it to go to trial?"

"It's looking that way." Sabre quit rubbing his shoulders.

"Thank you," JP said. "You're an angel."

Sabre pulled a chair close to JP and sat down. "Ron is still soul-searching, but I think he's close to a decision. He really wants to do what's best for Liberty, so I need to make sure I have all my ducks in a row. The subpoenas are all out, and I'm ready with my line of questioning. I just need to work on my closing argument a little more."

"You seem to be stressing over this more than usual."

"I've never defended an issue like this before. Not only that, it's personal. It's funny how much harder it is when you're closer to the client. I've had cases where I've gotten too attached, especially to some of the kids, and I've had to take a step back, but this is different. He's my big brother, and I can't let him down."

"I should be rubbing your shoulders."

"Thanks. But I'm meeting my mother at one, and she's treating me to a massage. So, what are you doing today?"

"Right now, I'm working on the Harn case. They sure didn't find much in the search yesterday."

"Because there wasn't anything to find. I'm still upset about that warrant. That was weak evidence. It sure didn't rise to the probable cause standard."

"I agree. I can't seem to find the missing piece in this case. There are so many suspects, but none seem to fit a premeditated scenario. I can see where any one of them could do it in the heat of the moment."

"Maybe someone went there to confront him, and things got out of hand."

"I considered that, but at this point, who would even go confront him?" Before Sabre could say anything, JP answered his own question. "Akroyd would be the most likely because he had just learned of his daughter's molest, but he's all alibied up. But it was likely someone Stadler knew because there's no forced entry. I've seen Akroyd. I wouldn't open the door to him late at night, not without my gun out of my holster. And we know Stadler was a coward."

"True."

"It could have been someone who had a key."

"Like Heidi," Sabre suggested.

"Or a young person who didn't appear to be a threat."

"You mean Opal."

"Or even one of the women from his past," JP said.

"You're not narrowing the field much, except that it leaves Tyler and Grady out."

"Unless Heidi and Grady were in cahoots. Although Wells thinks it was a one-person job."

"Heidi could've let Grady in and left. Or just given him a key."

"Well, that got us nowhere," JP said. "I've taken up enough of your time. I'll let you get to work."

"What are you going to do?"

"Talk to Thelma again. I have a couple of questions. And I've tried to call her several of times, yesterday and again this morning, and she's not picking up. I want to check on her."

~~~

JP knocked on Thelma's door, but no one answered. He was leaving, when Anne Green, the neighbor, walked past with her dog.

"If you're looking for Thelma, she left yesterday morning with her daughter."

"You haven't seen her since?"

"No. But she sometimes spends the weekend with her."

"Thank you. I'll check in with her on Monday."
~~~

Chapter 51

S

Saturday noon

JP was frustrated. He had nowhere else to go on the Harn case, and he felt like he was failing Sabre. The heat was on even though nothing had turned up in the search, at least nothing they knew about. He was stuck, so he decided to switch gears and spend some time looking for Izzy Hernandez' killer. He had gathered quite a bit of information from Natalie, including the names and addresses of two close friends, both hookers. That seemed the place to start.

He drove past the Naval Base to an apartment on Vesta Street in Barrio Logan where the first woman lived, a part of town saturated with sex workers. A lot of their business came from lonely sailors. The apartment complex was badly in need of maintenance and looked like it hadn't been painted in years. Little had been done to the outside, and there were few shrubs, just lots of dirty, oil-stained concrete. The apartment he approached had a torn screen on the window, and a hole loomed where the doorbell should've been. JP knocked, but no one answered. A scantily dressed woman with bright dyed-red hair and fingernails that matched strode over on sparkly high heels, smoking a cigarette. "You lookin' for Kristy?"

"Yep. Do you know where I can find her?"

"She's workin'." The woman took a long drag.

"Where would that be exactly?"

"You a cop?" The smoke escaped her mouth as she talked.

"I'm a friend of Natalie Hernandez. Her mother was Izzy Hernandez. Did you know her?"

"Yeah. Poor thing. What do you want with Kristy?"

"I'm a private investigator and I'm trying to find out who killed Izzy."

"I know who did it." She took another drag and blew it out. "We all know who did it."

"You do? Have you told the cops?"

"They don't listen."

"I'll listen."

She continued to smoke, talking between drags. "It was a john. Some rich, white guy, no doubt."

JP had never seen anyone smoke a cigarette so fast. It hardly left her mouth. "Do you have a name or description of the guy?"

"I just gave you a description. His name could be anything. I know the type."

He tried a few more questions, then realized she didn't have any real information about the killer, but she did tell him where he could likely find Kristy. He thanked her and left. He drove to the area on Dalbergia Street. Even though it was early in the day, several women were "working the streets." It didn't take long to spot Kristy Salome from the description Natalie had given—brown hair, five-foot-four, and very slight, but with ridiculously enhanced breasts and a full-on southern accent.

He introduced himself and explained why he was there. "I'd appreciate any help you can give us."

"I don't know much, darlin'. I seen her earlier in the evening, talked to her for a spell, but I wasn't here when she left."

"Do you know if she was picked up by anyone?"

"I heard she got into a fancy black car. No one seems to know what kind it was. The truth is no one pays that much attention."

"Did she seem her usual self when you saw her last? Anything out of the ordinary?"

"She seemed the same to me, sugar."

"Did she confide in you about anything going on in her life? Maybe about someone she was having trouble with?"

"No. But we didn't talk much about stuff. Susan knew her better."

"Susan Lokker?"

"That's it, darlin'. Have you already talked to her?"

"Not yet."

"You might wanna get right on that. She works more at night, so she's probably home now, but she might be asleep. She lives a few blocks from here. Do you need the address?"

"I have one, but maybe you can verify it." JP showed her the address, and she confirmed it was still good.

JP was at Susan's apartment within minutes. He rang the doorbell and a woman answered wearing a nightshirt. She was a bit rough around the edges, and on the long end of the business. She stood about five-foot-eight, and he could still see the blonde bomber in her tired, lined face and slightly baggy body.

When JP introduced himself, she said, "Natalie called me the other day. She said you might be coming by. Come on in."

JP stepped inside. "I hope I didn't wake you."

"Nah. I don't sleep that much." She led him to a counter that separated the kitchen from the living room and pointed to a barstool. "Have a seat."

She picked up a pack of gum from the counter and popped a piece in her mouth. "Want one?"

"No thanks."

They talked a bit about Natalie and Izzy. Susan had nothing but good things to say about Natalie. She was proud of the girl for finding her own way in life.

"How long did you know Izzy?" JP asked.

"About ten years. She was good people. She was a great mother, except she couldn't handle her drugs. They got the best of her. Most of us use somethin' just to get through this life, but you have to keep them in check and you have to be careful where you get them."

"You know she didn't die of an overdose, right?"

"Oh, I know she was strangled."

"Do you have any idea who might have done it?"

"You mean other than some crazy john? It's a risk with every client, even the regulars. You never know."

JP thought hooking sounded a lot like being a cop. Every call you went on, you wondered if you might meet your maker. And no one wanted you around unless they needed your services, and the public didn't respect you or even like you most of the time.

"I think I know what you mean." He smiled. "Was there anything going on in Izzy's life that might have triggered her murder? I mean, besides some random client." When she didn't answer right away, JP prompted her. "Anything different, even if it doesn't seem important."

Susan thought for a second. "I know she tried to get some rich guy to pay her hush money."

"Was he a client?"

"No. It was someone she knew many years ago, before she started in this business."

"Do you know what she had on him?"

"I'm not sure, but I know she lived with him in La Jolla for a short while when Natalie was young."

JP perked up. "Did he pay her when she asked for the money?"

"He gave her a hundred-dollar bill and told her he would meet up with her later."

"Did he?"

"I don't know."

"Did you ever see the man?"

"Just when we went to his house."

JP's pulse escalated. "You went to his house with her?"

"Yeah. That's when he gave her the money."

"Did you meet him?"

"No. I saw him from a distance. Even though the porch light was on, it was still kind of dark, so I couldn't see much. I waited in the car for her. I kept it running in case we had to make a quick getaway. That was my idea, not Izzy's. But nothing happened."

"You wouldn't happen to know the address, would you?"

"No. But I could take you there."

"When can you go?"

"If it'll help Natalie, I'll get dressed and we can go now."

"I really appreciate your help."

"I'd do anything for that girl. She's like a niece to me and she always treated me with love and respect."

JP drove to La Jolla, then followed Susan's directions. "Have you told any of this to the police?"

She shook her head. "Even though Izzy was dead, I didn't want to nark on her for trying to shake down some guy. And it didn't seem important at the time. She went to his house, got a hundred bucks, and that was the end of it. At least, I thought it was."

"How long after did Izzy disappear?"

"Just a few days." She sighed. "I guess I should've suspected him, but none of it seemed like a big deal at the time."

The streets they took on the way were very familiar to JP. He wasn't the least bit surprised when she told him to stop in front of Stadler's house.

Chapter 52

Monday morning

Sabre hitched a ride to work with JP because Ron's car was back in the shop, and he'd borrowed hers. Just as JP pulled up in front of the courthouse to let Sabre out, they saw a woman walking up to the door.

"That's Katherine Jackson," JP said. "She's one of the girlfriends who lived with Stadler for a while. Her daughter, Opal, was one of his victims."

"She's very attractive," Sabre said.

"I hadn't noticed."

"So, that's who you've been spending your time with. I'm not sure you should continue investigating this case." Sabre teased.

"You know I only have eyes for you, darlin'," he said lightly. Then his tone became more serious. "Why do you suppose she's here?"

"Maybe she's just visiting a friend. Or maybe she's having trouble with Opal, and CPS got involved."

"That doesn't seem likely."

"Maybe Opal has a delinquency charge."

"Katherine said she was doing very well."

"This is obviously bothering you. I'll check the calendar when I go in and see what I can find out. Last name is Jackson, right?"

"Right," JP said.

"Is Opal's last name the same?"

"As far as I know." He paused for a second. "Katherine told me she hasn't seen the father since before Opal's birth, so I'm guessing she gave the child her last name."

"I'll see you later." She leaned over and gave him a quick kiss, then exited the car.

Once inside the courthouse, Sabre looked around for Katherine. She was still looking when Bob approached.

"Hi, Sobs."

"Good morning."

"Who are you looking for?"

Sabre explained about Katherine. "I was just headed to the lounge. Come along and we'll check the calendar."

Bob looked over Sabre's shoulder as she checked the dependency calendar. "I don't see it," Sabre said.

"Nor do I."

"I'll check delinquency," Sabre said as they left the lounge. "Oh, there she is. That brunette over there by Department Three."

"Are you going to talk to her?"

"No. I don't want to spook her. I'll just check the calendar and see why she's here."

"I'll find out." He scooted off.

"Bob, get back here."

He turned. "Don't worry. I'll be discreet. Women love to talk to me."

Sabre sighed, walked up to the counter, and asked for the delinquency calendar. She soon found *Opal Jackson, Department Three, Attorney Alternate Public Defender Roberto Quiñones*. This wasn't Opal's first hearing and she was not with her mother, so Sabre guessed she was likely in Juvenile Hall. She wasn't sure what to do next. She could talk to Roberto and see what the charges were, but she didn't want to tip off Katherine. JP seemed to have a good relationship with her, but the woman obviously didn't want him to know about Opal's problems. So, she didn't want Katherine to think he was snooping around.

She was about to go find Roberto when Bob came back, grinning like a Cheshire cat.

"Spill," Sabre said.

"Her daughter, Opal, is fifteen. She's been hanging with the wrong friends and got busted for possession with intent to sell. Her attorney is working a deal to drop the intent charge and get her into a program. It sounded like a diversion."

"Is Opal in custody?"

"Yes, but her mom expects her to go home today."

"Do you know when she was arrested?"

"No. But it sounds like she's been in the Hall for a while."

Sabre went back to the desk and got the delinquency calendar again. She checked the date of arrest. *November 17th.*

Sabre called JP to give him the update.

He didn't take it well. "Her mother made it sound like she was doing great. She obviously isn't, and it upsets me that she lied."

"But at least you know it wasn't Opal. If she was arrested on the seventeenth, that was two days before Stadler was killed."

"That eliminates Opal, but it gives Katherine more of a motive if she blames Stadler for Opal's problems."

Chapter 53

Chapter 53

Monday afternoon

Sabre and Ron sat outside Department Four waiting for his case to be called.

"Are you sure this is what you want?" Sabre asked. "There's no going back once we do this."

"Yes," Ron said. "I'm certain. This is what's best for everyone, Liberty, Carla, Emma, and Roger."

"What about for you?"

"I think it's best for me too."

"You never cease to amaze me, Bro. You always think of yourself last." Sabre looked lovingly at her big brother. "Don't worry, this nightmare will be over soon."

"I'm no saint. I have selfish reasons too, but in the end, I believe it's what's best for my daughter." He gave Sabre a quick squeeze. "What happens now?"

"We call our witnesses, present everything to the judge, and wait for her decision."

"Any chance she won't rule in our favor?"

"There's always a chance, but I don't think so. The judge would have to do something pretty unconventional."

"Isn't that exactly how you describe Judge Hekman—as 'unconventional'?"

"She is, but she always wants what's best for the child, and I think she'll see that."

The bailiff stepped out and called the parties inside.

"It's show time," Sabre said.

"You're rather cavalier about this."

"Trust me. I know what I'm doing." Sabre felt a twinge as she said it. She believed Hekman would rule in their favor, but she was still a little nervous. The last thing she wanted was to let Ron know.

The case was called to order, and Judge Hekman sat silent for a minute just looking at the players. County Counsel Casey sat at one end of the table with the social worker, Laurie Snider. Next to her was Terry Chucas, the minor's attorney. Carla was next, then Bob, Sabre, and Ron. In the jury box were Emma and Roger Griffin where they could see and hear the proceeding.

Finally, the judge spoke. "Before we start, Mr. Clark, I know your client has had a rough few weeks. Is she in a good enough mental state to go forward today?"

"Yes, Your Honor. She is anxious to get this done, and she is on a medication that has stabilized her. She is feeling quite herself today."

The judge looked at Carla. "Is that correct, Ms. Larkin? Are you requesting that we do the trial today?"

"Yes, ma'am," Carla said. "It needs to be done. I'm fully aware what's going on and can make good decisions."

The judge cleared her throat. "I have to admit, I've never had a case quite like this. If no one objects, I'll start by granting *de facto* status to Roger and Emma Griffin."

Each of the attorneys agreed with the judge.

"The next issue is the paternity question and then the guardianship." The judge looked at Sabre. "Ms. Brown, this is your trial set. How do you want to proceed?"

"We're ready to go forward with the trial, Your Honor."

"There's no need for opening statements. Please call your first witness."

Sabre called Vaughn Ullman, the manager of the sperm bank, who testified that Carla worked there during the time Ron donated his sperm. Sabre also entered as evidence the contract Ron signed with the sperm bank, which stated he was giving up any legal rights to any offspring that were produced from his sperm.

"Why did Carla Larkin leave the employ of your company?"

"Objection," Bob said. "Speculation."

The judge turned to the witness. "Do you personally know why Ms. Larkin left the sperm bank?"

"Yes."

"Overruled," the judge said.

"Please answer the question," Sabre said.

"I asked her to resign," Ullman said.

"Why?"

"Objection." Bob said. "Relevance."

Sabre started to respond, but the judge cut her off. "I'll hear it. Go ahead, Mr. Ullman."

"We had reason to believe Ms. Larkin had pilfered the vials of sperm belonging to donor number 33323."

"And who is donor number 33323?"

"Ronald A. Brown."

"What brought you to the conclusion that Carla had taken the vials?"

"She was the last to handle the vials. She was the one who classified them and filed them."

"How soon after Mr. Brown's donation did you discover they were missing?"

"Six days after they were filed, someone chose number 33323, but when we went to retrieve the vials, they were gone. Empty vials had been put in their place."

"No further questions, Your Honor."

"County Counsel?" Judge Hekman said.

"No questions."

"Mother's attorney?"

Bob stood. "You didn't press charges against Carla, right?"

"Right."

"And you didn't file a police report, correct?"

"That's correct."

"In fact, you don't know for certain that Carla stole any vials of sperm, do you?"

"Not a hundred percent, but as close as I can get. She was the last to handle them before they went missing."

"Six days passed before you discovered they were gone?"

"Yes."

"No further questions," Bob said and sat down.

Sabre knew Bob was fishing for some doubt as to Carla's culpability. Since he didn't know what might come next, he was smart enough to stop. But Sabre knew.

"Any other cross examination?" the judge asked.

Both County Counsel and minor's attorney said no.

"Re-direct, Ms. Brown?"

"Mr. Ullman, in those six days could someone have taken the vials without anyone else knowing?"

"No."

"Why is that?"

"Because there are two keys to the storage unit where the vials are kept, and it takes both keys to open it. One key is readily available for the staff, and I have the other key."

"What if you're not there?"

"The sperm can only be obtained by appointment, so I'm always there."

Chapter 54

"Your next witness, Ms. Brown?"

"I'd like to call Emma Griffin."

Emma established that Carla had never gone anywhere for any length of time during the time of conception.

Bob asked questions that pertained to the guardianship, establishing their desire and ability to take care of the child.

"Ms. Brown?" the judge said.

"Your Honor, I have Deputy Marshal Newton available for video testimony."

"Proceed," the judge said.

Once the video was on and Newton came on, the clerk swore him in. Sabre asked a few questions about his background, then the other attorneys stipulated to his expertise in the WITSEC program. Sabre established that he was Ron's main contact during his time in the program, as well as the dates Ron was involved.

"Could Ron have made any trips to San Diego without your knowledge?"

"No. That wasn't possible. For the year preceding Liberty's birth, we knew at all times where Ron was. With Ron's agreement, and for his protection, we had him under constant watch. We tracked his phone, and Ron never went more than fifty miles from his home. Based on the age of the child, Ron could be Liberty's father unless the program was breached, and Carla came to see him."

Bob chose to cross examine Newton. "You did not spend every minute with Ron during his stay in the program, correct?"

"That's true."

"So, Ron could've been having a sexual relationship with someone and you wouldn't have known about it, right?"

"It's highly unlikely because we keep strong tabs on our witnesses, especially when other people come into their lives. The security is extremely tight."

"And yet, it was breached a few years ago by a woman Ron was having a relationship with. Is that correct?"

"That's true, but— "

Bob cut him off. "Ron also made a trip to San Diego after he had been in the program for five years, correct?"

"That's correct, —"

Before he could say "but," Bob said, "No more questions."

Sabre followed with re-direct. "Deputy Marshall Newton, how was that breach different from this situation?"

"That breach was done by highly trained professionals. We know for certain that Ron did not make any trips to San Diego except the one we arranged for him, and he was under watch twenty-four seven the entire time. Also, that trip took place a year before the child was born."

Judge Hekman glanced at Sabre. "Do you have any more witnesses, Ms. Brown?"

"I'd like to call my client to the stand for three questions."

"Three, huh?" Judge Hekman raised an eyebrow. "I may hold you to it."

"Three on direct. I can't guarantee that if I have to do re-direct."

"Please take the stand, Mr. Brown," Hekman said.

When Ron reached the witness chair, the clerk said, "Please state your name for the record."

"Ronald Adrian Brown."

"Please raise your right hand and repeat after me." The clerk swore him in and asked him to be seated.

Sabre asked her first question. "Did you at any time have a sexual relationship with Carla Larkin?"

"Yes," Ron answered.

"How long ago was your last sexual encounter with Ms. Larkin?"

"Over eight years ago."

"Did you ever give Ms. Larkin permission to use your sperm from a sperm bank?"

"No. I did not."

"No further questions."

"Does anyone want to cross-examine the witness?" The judge glanced from attorney to attorney.

County Counsel responded with, "No questions, Your Honor." As did Mr. Chucas.

The judge looked at Bob, who was conferring with his client. She waited as they whispered back and forth. Then Bob said, "No questions."

"The witness is excused." The judge nodded. "You may step down."

Ron walked back to his seat.

"Please call your next witness," Hekman said to Sabre.

"We have no further witnesses, Your Honor."

"Does anyone else want to call any witnesses?"

"No, Your Honor," came from both County Counsel and Bob.

"Then let's hear closing arguments. Ms. Brown?"

Sabre stood. "I want to start by emphasizing that my client does not take contesting this matter lightly. He never expected to find himself in this kind of dilemma, and he has given it a great deal of consideration. That said, as the court can see by the paperwork submitted, the biological father was under the belief that he would not have any responsibility for his sperm once the clinic took possession of it." Sabre glanced at her brother and then back at the judge.

"It's not as if the product he sold was defective and caused a problem. When he sold his sperm to the sperm bank, they assured him he no longer had a responsibility. I liken it to any other sale. If he'd sold a car to a dealership and four years later someone stole that car and had an accident, he wouldn't be liable for any damages. The evidence shows that Ron did not have sex with Carla during conception. Emma testified that Carla did not go out of town during that time, and Marshal Newton testified that Ron was being tracked and did not leave the state he was in. That leaves only one possible scenario. This child was conceived from Ron's sperm without him present. The only place he donated sperm was a clinic where Carla worked. Then Carla was fired when the sperm disappeared because she was suspected of taking the vials." Sabre paused to let all that solidify. Then she placed her hand on her brother's shoulder and continued.

"Mr. Brown has deep concerns for his child. He believes she has had enough confusion and chaos in her short life. He is confident that the Griffins will continue to provide her a good, stable home and that the child will still have contact with her mother whom she's quite attached to. If the court should find Ron is legally responsible, we would like to speak to the issue of guardianship." Sabre looked at her notes and read the applicable code section. "Until then, the California Family Code Section 7613 (b) (1) states: *The donor of semen provided to a licensed physician or to a licensed sperm bank for use in assisted reproduction by a woman other than the donor's spouse is treated in law as if the donor is not the natural parent of a child thereby conceived* ... Therefore, we submit on the evidence before the court and ask the court to find Mr. Brown has no *legal* responsibility to this child."

"Mr. Clark, would you like to make a closing statement?"

"No, Your Honor. My client wants to submit on the recommendations on both the paternity issue and the guardianship. She also offers a sincere apology for any chaos that she has caused due to her illness."

"Mr. Chucas?"

"It appears that Mr. Brown, although the biological father, has no legal responsibility to this child. We ask that the court grant a guardianship to the Griffins."

"County Counsel," the judge said, "please state the department's position on the record."

Casey stood and said, "It is our position that the biological father does not have a legal responsibility. As for the issue of guardianship, we ask for Liberty to be placed with the Griffins and a guardianship be granted."

Judge Hekman looked directly at Ron. "We seldom see this kind of situation for a man. Many young women have found themselves carrying a child because of a violation to their bodies. You did not have the physical trauma, nor did you have to carry the child inside you for nine months, so in that respect it is quite different. However, that does not mean you weren't violated. And the end result is a human being who needs love and caretaking. I believe Liberty receives that in the environment she is in, and I assume that played a major part in your decision. Mr. Brown, I don't know all your reasons for making the decision you did, but it appears that you have the best interest of this child in mind. For that, I commend you. And I find under Section 7613 (b) (1) of the California Family Code that you are not the legal father to Liberty Grace Larkin."

Sabre stood. "Your Honor, my client is concerned Ms. Larkin still possesses other vials of Mr. Brown's sperm. We have reason to believe there are still five vials that have not been used. We ask the court to order Ms. Larkin to return all those vials. Mr. Brown does not want to find himself in this position again."

The judge sighed and her shoulders dropped, obviously frustrated by the whole situation. "Carla Larkin is ordered to return any and all vials of sperm to Mr. Brown as soon as possible." She looked at the players at the table. "Anything else before I make a ruling on the guardianship?'

"No, Your Honor," each attorney responded in turn.

"Mr. Brown, you and your attorney are excused since you no longer have standing in this case."

Once outside the courtroom, Ron asked, "The judge will place her with Emma and Roger, won't she?"

"Absolutely. There's no reason not to, and everyone is in agreement. How are you feeling now that it's over?"

"I'm good with my decision. Emma told me she would keep me informed if I want to be. She's willing to treat it like an open adoption, if that's what I want."

"Have you considered it?"

"I have, but I don't think it'll work, especially with Carla still in the picture. I'll leave it up to Emma and Roger, and eventually Liberty, to come to me if life changes and it seems beneficial. Otherwise, I won't have any contact."

Sabre wasn't sure how she felt about it all. She agreed that it was probably best to not disrupt Liberty's life, but on the other hand, she'd just lost a niece.

Ron must have guessed what she was thinking because he said, "I know this affects you as well. How are you handling all of this?"

"I'm okay. I'm glad you didn't tell Mom. I don't think she would be able to not be involved."

"I know." He went silent for a few seconds. "You can still be a part of her life if you choose."

Sabre wrapped an arm through Ron's. "No, big brother, I think you're right. It would be too hard on all of us. Emma knows we're here if she ever needs us."

"I know the judge ordered Carla to return the unused vials, but she never admitted she had them. What's to keep her from doing this again?"

"We'll ask Bob when he comes out. Maybe he knows if there are any left."

"They're coming out now," Ron said.

Bob talked to Carla for a few seconds, then she left with Emma. He joined Ron and Sabre.

"What happened?" Sabre asked.

"The judge granted the guardianship."

"Any chance of getting my vials back?" Ron asked.

"Between us, Carla said to tell you there are three vials left. She had a total of nine, and it took her six tries to successfully impregnate herself. She has agreed to return the other three and will do so through her sister Emma."

"Emma said it took four tries. So, there should be five left."

"I don't know what to tell you about that. But Carla said there were three. I'll get whatever I can, and I'll push a little. If she does this again, she could get criminal charges, so I'll impress that upon her."

"Thanks, man."

"Don't worry, kid." Bob clasped Ron's shoulder. "Hey, it took her six tries last time, so chances are, she couldn't get another kid out of it anyway."

"That makes me feel a lot better," Ron answered sarcastically.

Chapter 55

Chapter 55

Tuesday morning

Ron arrived at the Silent Thunder Charity office at 8 a.m. ready to get started. He'd made a decision about Liberty and carried through. He was usually good at not second-guessing his decisions, but this one was tougher. He was confident he'd done what was right, but it still nagged at him that he wouldn't watch his child grow up.

Rose Marie walked into the office. "Are you ready to meet the others?" she asked.

"I'm ready. Who all is coming?"

"Sandy and Corina will be here in a few minutes. Is Sabre coming?"

"She's in court this morning."

"Then there'll just be the four of us. One day this week, maybe you can set up a meeting with Raleigh so you can get acquainted."

"That sounds good."

"Before the others get here, I'd like to go over a few things with you."

"Shoot."

"There was only one large gift made last year"—she raised one finger—"and there is quite a bit of money left in the budget for a second. It would be good if you could make a second gift before the end of the year to keep in line with Goldie's wishes."

"That doesn't give me a lot of time. What happens if I can't come up with one?"

"The money will carry over, but then you have to grant three next year." Rose Marie wagged three fingers. "It would be good to jump in and get your feet wet. It doesn't have to be huge, just something to see how it all works."

"You said the large gifts have to be board approved, how long does the process take?"

"The board has always been quick and seldom questioned Goldie's recommendations. I don't expect a problem for you either. You'll be fine if you locate a recipient who is worthy."

"I've read through the rules several times, so I think I'm ready to jump in."

A tall brunette woman about forty-five walked in. "We're ready to jump with you," she said. "I'm Sandy Barnes, your assistant."

"Thanks." Ron stood. "I'm Ron Brown. Nice to meet you."

"Likewise. I'm sorry about your aunt's passing. She was an incredible and extremely unique woman. I miss her a lot."

"Thank you. She was a special woman."

Corina came in a moment later. She was about the same age as Sandy with a similar thin physique, except she was blonde. She also commented on Goldie's amazing personality. Ron hoped he could fill his aunt's shoes.

They discussed the remaining budget for the year. "I won't go into all the details," Corina said. "I've emailed you an accounting for the year, so you can look that over, and if you have any questions just call me. As for the amount available for a big gift, there's around five hundred and sixty thousand still left. You don't have to spend it all. In fact, it would be good if you didn't, because the market has been fluctuating a lot. But I have every confidence in our stockbroker."

"Do you have a recipient in mind for a gift?" Sandy asked.

"I've been thinking about it a lot, and I may know someone who deserves it," Ron said. "What do I do once I find someone?"

"You have to investigate, of course, to make sure he or she qualifies, no current drugs or criminal history, etc. Then you file a report clearing your candidate and make your request. There's a simple form you fill out, either electronically or on paper. I'll email it to you."

"Thanks."

"The most important thing is that you use your heart to pick the recipients. I'm sure you'll do fine," Rose Marie said.

"Since it's all anonymous," Ron asked, "how is the money delivered to the recipient?"

"I help with that," Sandy said. "It all depends on the gift. Sometimes we pay things directly to an organization and remain anonymous. Sometimes, it's a more difficult situation. Most of the time, I'll be able to handle it. You may have to write a letter of explanation. Of course, you'll sign the letter IA, for Incognito Angel. Sometimes you may have to request permission from the recipient. This happens with schools, because you need to make sure the student is accepted and actually wants to attend. That can get a little tricky, but we'll manage."

When everyone left, Ron called JP. "Did you do a background check on Natalie Hernandez?"

"I did a criminal check," JP said. "Why?"

"Because I'm thinking about having the Incognito Angel buy her a new car and pay for her beauty school, but I need to do a background check on her."

"I know she has no criminal history, not even a parking ticket. What else do you need?"

"To make sure she isn't using illegal drugs or excessive alcohol."

"That shouldn't be too hard. You've done it for me, and those classes you took should come in handy. If you need any help, I'll pitch in."

"Thanks."

"By the way, I think it's great you're considering Natalie. She's had her share of bad luck, and she keeps pushing forward. I think she's the kind of person Goldie had in mind."

"I have to figure out how to do all this. What kind of car do I get her? I don't want to buy her something she doesn't like."

"She drives a clunker now. She'll be happy with anything she gets. Just find something reliable that gets good gas mileage, and she'll be happier than a turtle on an escalator."

Chapter 56

Chapter 56

Tuesday morning

JP spread out his paperwork across the dining room table—reports, charts, timelines, the photo of Thelma and her husband. He read through everything looking for the missing piece. He concentrated on his interview notes, carefully considering each motive and opportunity. Suddenly, he remembered something, but he had to verify it. He called Thelma, but she didn't answer. On a hunch, he started calling hospitals, posing as her brother. Thirty minutes later, he was on his way to Scripps.

Thelma was alone when JP walked into her room. She was hooked up to an IV and blood-pressure monitor. She looked surprisingly healthy and peaceful lying there with her eyes closed. He watched for a few minutes and thought about what an amazing woman she was. When she opened her eyes, she smiled at him.

"It's about time," she said.

JP wondered if she knew who he was. "It's JP. Remember me?"

"Of course, I remember you. What took you so long to get here?"

He still wasn't sure about her cognitive state, so he asked about something very familiar to her. "How is Camden?"

"He's fine. My daughter is keeping an eye on him."

"How are you feeling?"

"I'm having a good day, but it comes and goes."

JP stepped closer to her bed. "I hope you don't mind that I stopped by."

"I'm glad you did." She made an effort to smile and look relaxed. "I was afraid I was going to have to send for you."

"I'm here now, and it's my pleasure."

"I enjoy your company. You don't treat me like I'm fragile or a senseless old woman."

"You're far from either of those things. And you've led an interesting life."

"I've certainly done most of the things I wanted to do. I had the love of my life for many years. I have a great daughter and perfect grandchildren. I've had opportunities that many women don't get, and I'm grateful for that."

"And now you've accomplished everything you need to before you leave this earth." JP meant it as a statement, not a question

She responded with a conspiratorial smile. "You're a smart young man, JP. How did you figure out what you think you know?"

"It was a lot of little things."

"Have a seat and tell me. I want to know. Just don't expect me to admit to anything."

JP grabbed a chair and placed it next to her bed.

Thelma raised herself to a sitting position. "Now, talk to me."

"As I said, it was a lot of things that didn't add up. Your concern for Katherine and Opal, Opal's behavior, the statues, the photos on your mantel, the destroyed train room, easy access to Stadler's house, and the bruises on your face that you blamed on a fall."

"Go on."

"I think you suspected what was going on way back, and I'm guessing your suspicions grew with each new family. You kept adding to your playground, hoping to get the girls away from him, or at least give them a happy place to go. You felt guilty because you couldn't do more." JP watched her facial expressions and her occasional nod of the head. "How am I doing so far?"

"I had my suspicions about that man," Thelma said. "I wanted to call CPS, but I could never establish anything concrete. None of the girls, or their mothers, actually confided in me." She winced, reaching her hand up to her head.

"Are you okay?"

She swallowed. "Just a little pain. It comes and goes." She reached for JP's hand. "Do you mind?"

"My pleasure."

"Please go on."

"You got very attached to Katherine and Opal. They were like another daughter and grandchild. You made sure they got into therapy when they left. I'm guessing either Valerie did it for free or you paid for it."

"She did it for free."

"Because she would do anything for her mother, right?"

"She's a wonderful woman. When did you figure out our connection?"

"It took longer than it should have. When I met Valerie, she looked familiar. I didn't realize until this morning that it was because of the photo you have of her on the mantel. I was told her last name was Ellison, and even though it changed to Carter, it didn't mean much. Carter is a common surname and I mistakenly thought she'd got married, but I was wrong about that, wasn't I?"

"Yes."

JP continued. "Instead, she got a divorce and took back the name of her adoptive parents—Carter. You told me your daughter got a divorce, but I had no reason to connect the two things. You also told me you took in foster children and adopted one. Now, when I see all the pieces, I'm frustrated that I didn't figure it out sooner."

"You weren't looking for that kind of a connection, that's why." She closed her eyes again and squeezed JP's hand. When the pain passed, she said, "Tell me more."

"Katherine pretended that Opal was doing fine, but then I discovered Opal was using drugs. That started me thinking, so I went through everything again. When Dakota was removed from the home, your suspicions were confirmed. On top of that, I think Katherine confided in you about Opal's troubles. Perhaps you thought Stadler's death would give Opal some peace of mind. So, you decided you had to do something about it, something you wished you'd done years ago."

She squeezed his hand forcefully, the pain lasting much longer this time.

"Can I call to get you something?" JP asked.

"Nothing helps except morphine and that makes me groggy. I want what time I have left to be lucid. I can bear the pain. It always passes. So, until they come too close together, I'm okay." She smiled, but it looked forced. "Please keep going."

"I think the guilt for not being able to do something to help those little girls, combined with the pent-up anger you felt after hearing about Opal was just too much. You had been diagnosed with a fatal illness and knew you wouldn't likely be charged or wouldn't have time to suffer the consequences. You knew Stadler would be alone that night because Heidi told you she would be gone. You went over to his house, knowing he was alone, and confronted him. He let you in because he didn't feel physically threatened by a mature woman like you."

This time her smile was genuine. "You're very kind. Mature is a nice word."

"I'm not sure what happened after that. Maybe you intended to kill him, maybe not. Personally, I'd like to kill every pedophile that walks this earth, so maybe ..." Another hard squeeze, as her face contorted with pain. JP wanted to help but knew he couldn't, so he just waited. When she relaxed, he asked, "How did I do?"

"I will not admit or deny anything at this point, but you will know it all in due time."

"I would really like to know what the weapon was."

"And I'm sure when you find that, you'll have all the answers." She took a deep breath and blew it out slowly. "Will you promise me something?"

"Sure, if I can."

"I want you to attend my memorial service. It'll be graveside only and very small. I've left instructions that it be by invitation only. Your name is on the list."

"I promise, and if that ain't a fact, God's a possum."

She chuckled, then said, "It won't be long now."

"Is there anything else I can do for you?"

"No. I've said my goodbyes to the people in my life who mean the most, and I've asked to go home. That's where I choose to die. I'm lucky; not everyone gets to make that choice. Valerie will stay with me, and hospice is all set up. When the pain gets unbearable, they'll dope me up, and I'll either leave this earth or I won't care."

JP was captivated that she still had her wit, but he was out of words. She squeezed his hand hard again and her whole body jerked. When it stopped, she said, "Thank you for coming to see me. Don't worry, I've made sure your client does not go down for this."

"I appreciate that."

She let go of his hand. "Now go. Valerie will be here soon to pick me up, and I'm tired and need some rest."

Chapter 57

A week later

The cemetery was well kept. The service was to be held near the plot where Thelma's husband was buried. JP arrived before any of the family. He stood quietly in front of the tombstone with the epitaph *The World Is Diminished Because He Is Gone, But It's Still A Better Place Because He Was Here.* A second stone stood next to Oliver's with Thelma's name on it.

JP moved back from the gravestones so the family could get closer and watched as others arrived. He looked around at the small gathering of family and friends and wondered why he'd been included. He caught Katherine's eye as she walked up. When she and Opal joined him, she introduced them. Opal was thin, but she looked and talked as if she might have been clean. JP hoped he was right. When Opal stepped away to greet Valerie, Katherine said, "She's doing well. We have a long road ahead, but she's really trying. I have high hopes."

"One day at a time."

"That's what she's doing. She's taking her therapy and meetings seriously."

"Good," JP said. "Do you know any of these people? The only one I know is Valerie."

"Those two adult men are Thelma's children, and the rest are their wives and kids.

The only other people were three older ladies in red hats. "And those women?"

"I'm guessing her bridge club. Thelma belonged to the Red Hat Society, and I know her bridge friends did as well."

Valerie walked to the front and everyone grew silent. She cleared her throat and began.

"Each of you are here today because you were important to my mother. She was loved by so many and would've had a very large crowd if we had let others know. But that's not the way she wanted it. She only wanted those who really knew her heart and soul." Her daughter cleared her throat. "Per her request, we are gathered by Daddy's gravesite because my mother said she couldn't wait another minute to be with him. They had a love that transcended time."

"My mother had three missions in life. One was to be a good wife, which I'm sure she was because Daddy always seemed so happy when he was with her. Second, she strove to be a good mother and grandmother. We can certainly attest to that. She made each of us feel like we were her favorite. Third, she wanted to protect little children from the evils of this world. She decided early on that the best way to do that was to take in foster children, which she did for many years." Valerie looked at JP, then continued. "If she could have, she would've rid the world of bad guys, so God's little children could walk this earth without fear."

Did she know what her mother did? JP wondered. He didn't think Thelma would have told her because that would have made her an accessory. But she may have figured it out.

Valerie went on to say how she had been given a home by an amazing woman. "I had a mother before who I barely remember, but this is the mother God sent me. She was my savior, and I loved her with all my heart. The day I came to her house was the day my life really began. That's the date we used to celebrate my birthday. My mother was the strongest, bravest woman I've ever met. She lived every minute of her life for each of us." Valerie looked up at the sky. "You take care of her now, Daddy. Your love is home at last, and I know you're together, waltzing in the stars."

After the service, Valerie approached JP and asked him to walk to her car. She handed him a taped box about eighteen inches square, with his name written on the top. "My mother wanted you to have this. She made me promise to give it to you, then assured me you would be here today to collect it. She also said something about a possum that made absolutely no sense."

JP laughed. "Of course, she did."

~~~

JP carried the unopened box into the house, and Sabre greeted him with a kiss.

"How was the service?" she asked.

"It was very nice. Short and sweet, just like her."

"What's in the box?"

"I don't know yet. Thelma instructed her daughter Valerie to give it to me at the service. That must be why she wanted me there."

"She could've had you pick it up anywhere. She took a shining to you."

JP took out a small pocketknife and cut the tape. Inside the box on top of a sheet of tissue paper were two sealed envelopes. One was addressed to *JP Torn*; the other to *Detective Wells*. He laid the envelopes aside and pulled back the tissue paper. "Well, slap my head and call me silly." There it was in all its glory—one of the dragon statues he'd been searching for. It was in a clear plastic bag. JP removed it from the box and set it on the table. Then he removed the other plastic bag, which contained a model train car.

"That's the statue in the photograph with Oliver and Thelma," Sabre said. "And the boxcar the police thought was missing?"

"My guess is that one or the other is the murder weapon."
~~~

JP opened the envelope addressed to him and pulled out a three-page, handwritten letter.

Sabre said, "Read it out loud."

JP began:

My Dear JP,

First, I want to tell you how much I appreciated your visits. I was able to tell you stories from my past that my family was tired of hearing. You are such a great listener. I appreciate the work you do for children. Like you, I can't stand to see children suffer. It has always been my goal to help as many as I can. Unfortunately, I failed to protect Ritchie's victims and for that, I'll be forever haunted. Well, I guess not for long since I won't be around much longer. (I hope you appreciate the humor.)

The other envelope, which I expect you to give to the homicide detective, contains my confession. I killed Ritchie Stadler. I explained how I took the statue over to his house. I figured if Ritchie didn't want to let me in, he surely would when he saw the dragon. I held it up so he could see it through the peephole. I was right. He opened the door. I told him that I knew what he had been doing to those innocent little girls, and that he would finally go to prison and that I would happily testify to everything I had seen over the years. But he wasn't even listening to me. All he wanted was to get his hands on the stupid statue. Finally, he started screaming at me, calling me a crazy old lady. Then he lunged at me, and I swung the dragon at him, and he fell to the floor.

I checked his pulse, and he was still breathing. I was going to call an ambulance, but when I looked over, I saw that horrifying train room that I had come to suspect he used to lure so many innocent children. I went in there and started swinging the statue at the trains. The next thing I knew, Ritchie grabbed my hand and took the statue from me. He swung it at me, but he was off balance and he missed. I grabbed a boxcar and when he came at me again, I hit him as hard as I could. He staggered around for a bit, and then just fell to the ground.

When I checked his pulse that time, there was none. So, I picked up the statue and the boxcar and left.

I need you to deliver these things to Detective Wells, along with his letter. My fingerprints and Ritchie's will be on them, as well as his DNA. There shouldn't be any questions left as to who did this, and your client will be cleared.

In case you're wondering, this is not the statue Katherine had. She told me you were asking about it. This is the twin, the one that disappeared years ago. It was taken by Baby Belle, which is what I called Belle's daughter. She gave it to me. At the time, I was going to return it, but I set it aside and forgot about it. Then when Belle left, I was afraid if I gave it back to Ritchie, he would go after her and maybe press charges against Belle, so I just kept it hidden away. I don't know if Katherine still has hers or if she knows how valuable it is. Maybe you could let her know, and she can get some financial compensation for what he did.

JP, I want you to know that I intended to kill Ritchie. He ruined so many lives, he didn't deserve to live. Maybe he would've gone to prison, but likely not for long and I don't think that would've helped Opal or any of his other victims. And then he would've been free to hurt more innocent little girls. I couldn't leave this earth knowing that. But please do me a favor. Make sure Valerie and the others believe I had no intent. I think it would be easier for them. What the police believe doesn't matter much to me, but it's important to me that my family is at peace with it. I can't say I'm sorry it happened. Maybe I'm wrong, but I don't think any merciful God will punish me for it.

Don't mourn for me. I'm waltzing through the universe in the arms of the man I love.

Thelma

"That didn't come any too soon," Sabre said.

"I know. Wells told me they were closing in on our client. He may have been just pressuring me to find out what else I knew. It worked. I was starting to think I had to dump everything on him to keep Harn from being arrested. Thelma told me I would know everything soon, so I've been waiting to see if she might have had something sent to me. And she did."

Chapter 58

Six days later

JP, Sabre, and Ron ordered food from Natalie at Maritza's and then took a seat.

"Did you take Thelma's confession to Detective Wells?" Ron asked JP.

"Yes. After he investigated, he decided to close the case since everything she said seemed to fit in place."

"Did he clear Grady?"

Sabre smiled and said, "He sure did. He's already started unsupervised visits and we should have Dakota home with her father before Christmas."

"I'm glad to hear that."

"Did you get the tuition all set up?" Sabre asked.

"Yes," Ron said. "I sent the letter to Natalie offering beauty school tuition at Paul Mitchell—The School. She had already applied and been accepted. They were just waiting for the money, which Sandy set up and Corina paid. The tuition was about twenty thousand, plus another two grand for books and supplies. She'll still have to work to pay for her rent and food. But after today, she won't need to spend money on her vehicle. We're also paying her car insurance while she's in school."

"You're sure the car will be delivered today?" JP asked.

"It's all set up. The dealership is bringing it here." Ron checked his watch. "In about ten minutes."

Natalie walked over to their table with a tray of food. She set each plate down, naming the entree as she did. After she set the salsa on the table, she said, "I want to thank you guys."

"For what?" JP asked.

She shrugged. "I don't know exactly, but it seems my luck changed when you came into my life."

"How so?"

"You found my mom's murderer, and even though he will never pay for it, at least not on this earth, he got what was coming to him. And I'm relieved that he's not walking free. I don't know how you did that, and so quick, but I'll be forever grateful."

"You did it," JP said. "You didn't give up and you gave me the information I needed. The rest was a little skill and a lot of luck. I just happened to draw a pat hand from a stacked deck."

Natalie had a light in her eyes that none of them had seen before. "On top of that, The Incognito Angel paid my tuition for beauty school, and I'm sure it was you two who left me that hundred-dollar bill in the tip jar. I was able to get a new battery for my car with it, so I have transportation again, at least for now."

"I don't know anything about a tip," JP said. "Do you, Ron?"

"Nope, but I'm happy for you, Natalie."

"I didn't even know about the Incognito Angel until I got the letter," Natalie continued. "I thought it was a hoax until my friends told me differently. Everyone seemed to know about the charity, but me. I guess I should read the newspaper. Have you heard of him or her?"

"Yeah," Sabre said. "She's been around for a few years now, spreading joy. I say 'she,' because it sounds like something a woman would do. A reporter has been trying to pin her down, but I hope he doesn't succeed because that might put an end to it all. She has done so much for so many deserving people."

"I've been reading all about her online. And it is real. My tuition is paid, and I start school in two weeks. I can't wait."

A middle-aged man in a suit walked into Maritza's. He looked around the tiny restaurant and spotted Natalie, then walked up to the table.

"Are you Natalie Hernandez?"

"Yes." Her voice sounded a little shaky, obviously not sure what to expect.

He handed her an envelope with her name scrawled on the front.

"What's this?"

"Read it," he said. "It's not a bad thing."

She opened the envelope and read it to herself. Then she looked up with a confused expression. A hesitant smile started to slowly form on her face.

"What does it say?" Ron asked.

When she started to read it aloud, a hush came over the room. The four customers were all staring. The cooks came out from the back, and Carmen, her boss, took her side.

Dear Natalie,

This should help you get back and forth to school. Have a nice life, and do a little act of kindness for others whenever you can.

IA

The man in the suit handed her keys.

"Wh...what is it? Where is it?" She glanced out the glass front of the café and waved her arms, uncertain.

"It's a brand-new Toyota RAV4 XLE Hybrid. The color is ruby flare pearl, and it's parked outside." He was still talking when she ran for the door. "With ash interior."

The man followed her outside, along with Carmen and most of the customers. Ron, Sabre, and JP stayed inside because cell phone cameras had come out and too many photos were being taken.

"Being here may not have been such a great idea," Ron said.

"Yeah," Sabre agreed. "We need to re-think that for next time."

"But it sure was amazing to watch," Ron said.

"If that girl was any happier, she'd have to hire somebody to help her enjoy it."

From the Author

Dear Reader,

Thank you for reading my book. I hope you enjoyed reading it as much as I did writing it. Would you like a FREE copy of a novella about JP when he was young? If so, scan the QR code below and it will take you where you want to go. Or, if you prefer, please go to www.teresaburrell.com and sign up for my mailing list. You'll automatically receive a code to retrieve the story.

Teresa

Made in United States
Orlando, FL
25 February 2026

78759042R00150